For Arthur and Vicki ~
With much love,

Frank.

THE GLUMS

Supplied under copyright from London Weekend Television

THE GLUMS

Based on the original radio scripts by

FRANK MUIR &
DENIS NORDEN

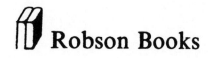 Robson Books

The publishers are grateful to the Vintage Magazine Shop for making available much of the original 'fifties material which has been used to illustrate this book.

FIRST PUBLISHED IN GREAT BRITAIN IN 1979 BY ROBSON BOOKS LTD.,
28 POLAND STREET, LONDON W1V 3DB. COPYRIGHT © 1979 FRANK MUIR AND
DENIS NORDEN.

Muir, Frank
   The Glums.
   I. Title
   II. Norden, Denis
  822'.9'14   PN6175
  ISBN 0-86051-080-8

Designed by Timothy Jaques and Harold King

Printed in Great Britain by The Garden City Press Ltd., Letchworth, Herts SG6 1JS

Contents

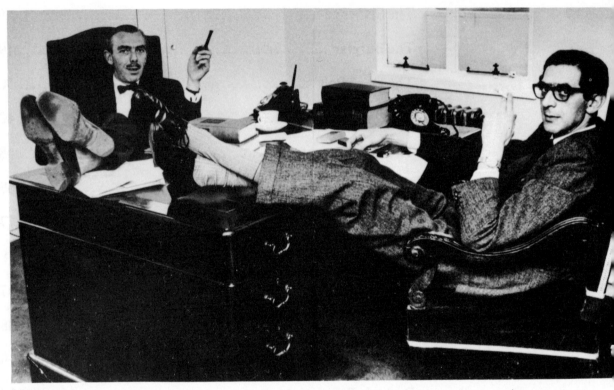

Frank Muir and Denis Norden, 'fifties style.

(Popperfoto)

Preface

Twenty-five years ago, when we were writing *Take It From Here* for the wireless and were as usual stuck for an idea, it occurred to us that as the air-waves were becoming clogged with everyday stories of good-hearted, decent folk like the Archers and the Huggetts (remember *Meet the Huggetts?*) we might redress the balance by writing the everyday doings of a really *awful* family. We called them the Glums. Mr Glum was the original male chauvinist swine; boozy, sentimental, bullying, and selfish. He was fiercely possessive of his son Ron and beastly to his wife and to his son's fiancée, Eth. Ron was as thick as a post and Eth was a very plain girl who was desperately loyal to Ron who represented her one chance of getting married.

The Glum stories ran for the rest of the natural life of *Take It From Here* and became its most popular segment. Possibly because the characters were so superbly played by Jimmy Edwards, June Whitfield and Dick Bentley. Perhaps because the stories and the humour closely reflected the rapidly crumbling moral values and attitudes of life in the nineteen-fifties.

One tradition which was still holding firm in the 'Fifties was the lengthy 'engagement' and much of the Glum comedy was based upon this curious social contract. In those days Ron and Eth would have begun by 'going friends', progressed to 'walking out' and ended up by becoming 'engaged'. Because they could not afford to get married the state of being 'engaged' became a kind of substitute. It gave the couple a bit of status and also allowed them, even in those unpermissive days, a fraction more licence. Ron, who had an occasional faint stirring of the flesh, made the odd lunge at Eth, but she, a true daughter of the 'Fifties, would have none of it while she was still unwed. Being engaged in those days was put variously as 'being given a present for Christmas and not being allowed to open it until Easter', and 'driving with one foot on the brake and the other on the accelerator'.

When *Take It From Here* came to an end in 1958 that seemed to be the finish of the Glums. But twenty years later, in 1978, a deeply intelligent young television producer called Simon Brett took it into his head to put the Glums on television, with Jimmy Edwards playing Mr Glum, Patricia Brake playing Eth and Ian Lavender as Ron. The original scripts were used and the sets and clothes were firmly of the mid 'fifties. Although the Glums were only part of a long and complicated show, and the show itself was not a success, the Glum sketches were a hit.

The Glums were back. London Weekend Television decided to give them a television series to themselves using two stories a week to make up the half hour. But what had happened to those original scripts? We had to ransack BBC archives, filing cabinets, cupboards and tool sheds before we had enough dog-eared, yellowing scripts to hand over to the actors.

Here are some of those scripts — in print for the first time.

Frank Muir

Denis Norden

THE SIXPENCE

The pub, night. Pub hubbub, over which:

LANDLORD: *(shouting)* Time, gentlemen, please. All your glasses, please. On your way please, gents. Drink up, Mr Glum. 'Ere, Mr Glum, why you been sitting there all night looking so disconsolate?

MR GLUM: Because, Ted, I have no reason to be looking consolate. In fact, if anything — look, Ted, you've known me a long time. You know what it is I love more than all the treasures of this earth?

LANDLORD: Oh, I do, Mr Glum. And, quite frankly, I think you've had enough of it for one —

MR GLUM: Not my beer! My son! My Ron.

LANDLORD: Ron?

MR GLUM: You *know* him! 'Course you do! Don't you remember that night when the police had to come here to remove a customer for molesting your barmaid?

LANDLORD: . . . Yes.

MR GLUM: Well, Ron was the one who ran after 'em shouting 'Let go my Dad!' And, as you may also recall, he's got this fiancée, Eth.

LANDLORD: *(trying to place her)* Eth . . . ?

MR GLUM: Oh, come on — she's round here practically every Saturday night.

LANDLORD: The one who carries your *feet*?

MR GLUM: That's her! That's the girl. A bit like Sophia Loren.

LANDLORD: *(doubtfully)* Sophia Loren?

MR GLUM: Well, if you can imagine a short, blonde, dumpy Sophia Loren. And, what you must also be aware, Ted, is that him and her have been engaged for quite some time.

LANDLORD: Yes, they have, haven't they? *Quite* some time. I should think your Ron's been going out with that Eth now for . . . ooh . . . for *what* is it?

MR GLUM: Well, whatever it is, I don't think he's got it. In fact, sometimes I wonder about him altogether. To be quite truthful, Ted, I get to believing that what's happened with Ron is perhaps his physical body has grown too big for his mental brain. The same fate as overtook the dinosaur.

LANDLORD: How'd you mean?

MR GLUM: Well, put another brown in there and I'll give you a for-example. Take what emerged when him and Eth were bashing our sofa-springs last Tuesday —

Music, and we hark back to the Glums' sitting-room, Tuesday night.

Ron and Eth are on the sofa.

ETH: Oh, Ron ... don't think I'm trying to pry, but — is everything all right? I mean, the whole evening you've been sort of wrought-up. Have you got anything at all on your mind?

RON: No, Eth.

ETH: Dearest, I don't want to appear to doubt your word, but ... that hammer. Every time you think I'm not looking, you go over to the mirror and hit yourself on top of the head with it. Beloved, I think I'm entitled to ask — why?

RON: (*pause, then obviously lying*) My bed's too short.

ETH: ... You're fibbing, aren't you, Ron?

RON: Yes, Eth.

ETH: Dearest, unless you confide in me, I can't help you. And if you want my opinion, this hitting yourself on top of the head with a hammer indicates you're in a very highly strung state of tension. You do get that in sensitive people. So, Ron, you're *going* to tell me, whether you like it or not.

RON: All right, Eth.

ETH: Well?

RON: I *don't* like it, Eth.

ETH: Then why keep doing it, dearest heart?

RON: I've got to, Eth. It's the only way to — solve my problem.

ETH: Ah! So there *is* a problem! I *thought* you wouldn't keep hitting yourself on top of the head with a hammer unless there was some good reason. Dearest, won't you let me help you?

RON: If you like, Eth. (*He hands her the hammer*)

ETH: Not hit you — solve your problem.

RON That *will* solve it, Eth. If I'm hit on top of the head with a hammer long enough — I won't have my problem.

ETH: You won't have your head, either. Ron Glum, you are going to tell me here and now — what kind of problem has made you take to hitting yourself on top of the head with a hammer? Is it ... some form of guilt?

RON: No, Eth.

ETH: Family trouble?

RON: No, Eth.

ETH: An — (*biting her lip*) — affair of the heart?

RON: No, Eth.

ETH: Then *what*?

RON: ... I've got a sixpence stuck up my nose.

ETH: You've ... Oh, Ron!

Over her appalled wail, we bring in music. When we return to the scene, it's an hour later.

Ron is now standing up, with Eth behind him holding his head steady — while, in front of him, Mr Glum is crouching, shining a torch up his nose.

MR GLUM: Just keep his head tilted back, Eth. (*Peering*) I got a definite *glint* then. Ah, yes! Yes, I can see the tanner.

ETH: Which side is it?

MR GLUM: Tails.

ETH: Which side *nostril*?

MR GLUM: The left-hand one. Well, there's a thing, eh. (*Releasing Ron*)

Oh, Ron, you are a thoughtless boy. Do try and *remember* next time — when you're tossing for drinks — pull your head back.

ETH: That wasn't how he did it, Mr Glum. It was — oh, tell him, Ron.

RON: I — I don't like to, Eth.

MR GLUM: (*indulgently*) Oh, come on, Ron, no need to be scared. If it's happened, it's happened, no sense my being cross with you now. I'm just curious, that's all. Where'd the sixpence come from?

RON: It's yours, Dad.

MR GLUM: (*fury*) It's —! (*Threatening him with torch*) I'll *maim* him! I'll give him such a tanning, he'll — *my* sixpence! (*Seizes Ron*)

RON: No, Dad, don't!

MR GLUM: I'll teach you to play fast-and-loose with my earnings. (*Shaking Ron*) Give it back, do you hear me, give it back.

RON: No, Dad, don't!

ETH: Mr Glum, stop it! Let him go! You haven't *lost* your money — he's *got* it for you. It's still *there*.

MR GLUM: Are you trying to set him up as a sort of human home safe? I *need* that sixpence, Eth. I got to have its purchasing power.

ETH: You will, Mr Glum. If you'll just let Ron tell you how the sixpence got *in*, it might help how to get it out. Now, what were you saying, Ron?

RON: I was saying, 'No, Dad, don't.'

ETH: Before that, beloved. How it happened.

RON: Well — tea-time, Dad gave me a shilling to get him sixpennorth of chips. At the fish shop. So the man gave me the chips and a sixpence change. Then I remembered. Dad likes vinegar sprinkled over.

MR GLUM: Gives the newspaper a better flavour. You still haven't told us what made you put the sixpence inside your nose.

RON: I should think that would have been obvious. How else could I pick up the vinegar-bottle? (*Demonstrates*) I had the chips in one hand and in the other hand I had the sixpence.

ETH: Couldn't you have put it in your pocket?

RON: No, Eth — it's chained to the counter.

ETH: Not the vinegar bottle. The *sixpence*! Why didn't you put the sixpence in your *pocket*?

RON: (*pause*) ... Anyone can be wise *after* the event.

MR GLUM: (*incredulous*) Do I understand that in order to handle the chips and the vinegar — you shoved the sixpence up your *nose*?

RON: Yes, Dad.

MR GLUM: (*helpless gesture*) I suppose we have to be thankful he didn't get sixpennorth of coppers. So then what d'you do?

PRINCESS MARGARET

This is Birthday Week for Princess Margaret. Twenty-one on August 21, the Princess now takes a full share in the Royal duties of her family. In this week's Picture-Story, ILLUSTRATED presents four years of her life when full rush of victory followed days of total war

1943 Margaret entered her teenage year at a time when the war was at its grimmest. For the girl who was to embody the spirit of youthful gaiety for postwar millions, routine at this time was sedate and austere. Windsor Castle formed an almost permanent background to her early growing. Not that she was overawed by her surroundings. On the contrary, she lightened the gloomier corners with her eager curiosity and bright shafts of wit. Frequently she would break down the stiffness of formal gatherings by darting unexpected questions, or by giving an unpremeditated and high-spirited wave instead of more customary royal styles of greeting

Millions bought the new £1 Savings Certificates issued in January. The sisters took along their pound notes

Thanksgiving Service for the North African victory. The Royal Family attended the St. Paul's ceremony

They were still digging for victory, helped by a cropping chart which they studied in Windsor garden

Informal outing for the Royal Family at Sandringham where the private golf course was ploughed up to produce a bumper crop of oats

RON: I walked home and I gave you the chips and you gave me one for going. Which I ate. Then — then I licked my fingers. First *this* finger, then th —

MR GLUM: All right, all right — never mind the human interest stuff. I just want the saline facts.

RON: Well ... Well, then I went upstairs and had my lie-down. And when I woke up, I suddenly thought — Ooh! What about Dad's sixpence? (*Pause*) Do you know, Eth, I looked *everywhere* for it!

ETH: (*incredulous*) You'd *forgotten* where you put it?

RON: Yes, Eth. (*Triumph*) And you'll never in a million years guess where I finally found it!

MR GLUM: (*bitterly*) Up your great stupid hooter!

RON: (*amazed*) Oh, Dad, you got it first time! It took me ages.

MR GLUM: (*gazing at him*) I dunno ... Sometimes it's hard to think of him as the end-product of millions of years of civilization.

ETH: Mr Glum, it's no good you just standing there with that expression of loathing. The deed's done. What about your son?

MR GLUM: *He's* going to be very soon.

ETH: This isn't the moment for recriminations, Mr Glum. If we don't get that coin out of there, it might — well, I don't want to be an alarmist — but one must think of it. That sixpence might travel.

MR GLUM: Travel?

RON: Oh, I don't think so, Eth. I heard Mum say a sixpence doesn't go *anywhere* these days.

ETH: That's not what I mean, Ron. I admit I don't know what one's nostril-tube is *connected* with — but surely there's the possibility. The sixpence might work its way up to the interior of Ron's head.

MR GLUM: That must be fascinating country. (*Irritable*) It's all very well saying get it out, Eth — but how?

ETH: (*acidly*) Well, you've never had any difficulty getting sixpences out of the gas-meter.

MR GLUM: (*angrily*) I do that from the *back* with a long bit of wire! (*Gazes at Ron's back for a moment, considering. Then —*) No, this is different, I suppose. It's a — here, wait a minute. Of course! (*Confidence*) I know how to dislodge it. A simple scientific principle.

ETH: How?

MR GLUM: Hit him on top of his head with a hammer.

ETH: He's been doing that since last night! It just doesn't work. Look ... surely there must be some way of *blowing* it down.

MR GLUM: Well, it's worth trying, I suppose. Shove my bicycle-pump nozzle in his ear, then —

ETH: No, no! *Ron* blow it. Beloved —

RON: Yes, Eth?

ETH: Listen. Place one finger hard against your good nostril ... that's right. Now blow as hard as you can down the sixpenny one. Go on.

RON: Right ... (*Blows hard and steadily*)

ETH: ... Anything happening, Mr Glum?

MR GLUM: Only that he's taking on a startling resemblance to Louis Armstrong. All right, give over, Ron.

RON: (*gasps, sags*)

MR GLUM: Grab him, Eth! Tell you what — while he's half-sparked out, lay him down. (*They lay Ron on sofa*) Now fetch me over the sugar-tongs. If I can just get a *purchase* on the coin. Just hold steady, Ron.

ETH: That's my brave soldier.

(*Mr Glum pushes sugar-tongs up Ron's nostril*)

RON: (*sharp howl of agony*) No, Dad, no! No! No! Ow!

MR GLUM: Oh, now don't make out that hurt! Baby you are! Really, sometimes you're a disgrace to your Dan Dare badge. (*Beckons Eth over; sotto*) Now, see if you can hold him while I pull the sugar-tongs out. Never imagined they'd go up so far. (*Seizes tongs, pulls*) Ah!

RON: (*moans softly*)

MR GLUM: All right, I'm sorry. But if you keep your head *still*, next time I might get it up the *correct* nostril.

ETH: No, Mr Glum, no. I really don't think you should any more. If the sixpence has to be got down like that, then it should be done by somebody — qualified.

MR GLUM: You mean, like — a sweep?

ETH: A doctor. A proper doctor. Mr Glum, you just get on to the cottage hospital — and tell 'em we've got an emergency.

Music and we go to the Casualty-room, Cottage Hospital.

A worried Surgeon greets the entering trio.

SURGEON: Don't worry, Mr Glum, as soon as I got your phone-call, I cleared two theatres. It's not often we get a disaster alert here, but I've cancelled all leave and two assistant surgeons are already scrubbing up. So, tell me — what exactly is this 'startling challenge to modern surgery' you mentioned?

MR GLUM: Sit down, Doctor, and conserve your strength for the task what lies ahead. I am a father who is putting all his faith in your professional skill. This 'ere is Eth — a girl whose married future depends on the magic of your healing hands.

SURGEON: (*indicating Ron*) And who is this?

RON: I'm the one who put the money up.

SURGEON: Put what money up?

MR GLUM: Steel yourself, Doctor. (*Break in the voice*) This young youth standing here, outwardly so brave and unconcerned, he — he ... (*Swallows, then resolutely*) Doctor, the time for mincing words is past. He's got a sprarzi up the snitch.

SURGEON: ... A what up the *what*?

ETH: His dear nose. There's a sixpence up there.

SURGEON: (*incredulous*) And for that you requested the whole Casualty Wing be put on emergency stand-by!

MR GLUM: Forgive an old man's anxiety, Doctor. You must remember I was speaking not only as the father of the boy — but as the owner of the sixpence.

SURGEON: I've never heard of such a waste of ... (*Impatiently*) Oh! (*Presses button of intercom*) Operating Theatre?

CONFIDENT VOICE: Standing by, Doctor.

SURGEON: Kill your lights! And bring me a pair of tweezers. Now, for goodness' sake, let's have a look at this nose. (*Peers up*) Mmm ... What are these abrasions on the *other* nostril?

MR GLUM: They're tong-marks.

SURGEON: Tong — ? You mean he's Chinese?

MR GLUM: No, he's always that colour. Comes of not eating his greens. Doctor, is there — is there hope?

SURGEON: (*scornfully*) Hope? To think I was hauled out of a Golf Dinner for this! For heaven's sake get outside, both of you.

Music, and we return to the Glums' sitting-room, later.

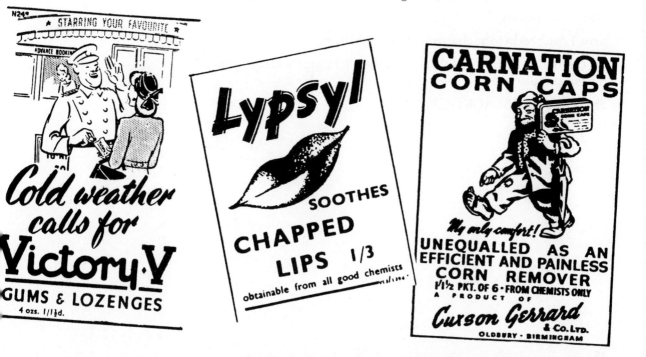

The trio are entering.

MR GLUM: And I still say the way that doctor carried on was most unprofessional. I've got a good mind to report his whole attitude to the BTM.

ETH: (*wearily*) Oh, Mr Glum, it's over now. The sixpence is out, so let's consider the episode closed. Please?

MR GLUM: Not quite closed, may I remind you, Eth. I'm still waiting for Ron to give me *back* that tanner.

ETH: For goodness' sake, Ron, give it him back and let's have done.

RON: Right ho, Eth. (*Feeling in pockets*) Now what did I do with it?

ETH: Oh, Ron — please.

RON: No, I've *got* it, Eth, I know that. I remember having it in my hand on the bus when that inspector came upstairs and asked to see all tickets, please. I remember that distinctly. I had my cap in *this* hand and the sixpence in *that* hand and I had to get my ticket out. So-o-o ...

ETH: Ron, Ron, you didn't —

RON: Oh, Eth! You really don't give me credit for any intelligence, do you? Do you really think I'd be so silly as to put it up my nose again after all that? Honestly, Eth! I may not be very clever but I don't make the same mistake twice.

MR GLUM: Well, where *is* it, then? (*Pause*) Where is it? ... Ron, I'm talking to you.

RON: Are you *talking* to me, Dad?

MR GLUM: (*shout*) 'Course I'm talking to you.

RON: You'll have to speak up, I'm afraid.

MR GLUM: Speak up?

RON: I don't seem to be able to hear out of this *ear*.

MR GLUM: Out of this ... ? Oh, no! Get the pliers, get the tongs! Where's my long bit of wire?

Playout music and BLACKOUT.

THE BURGLAR

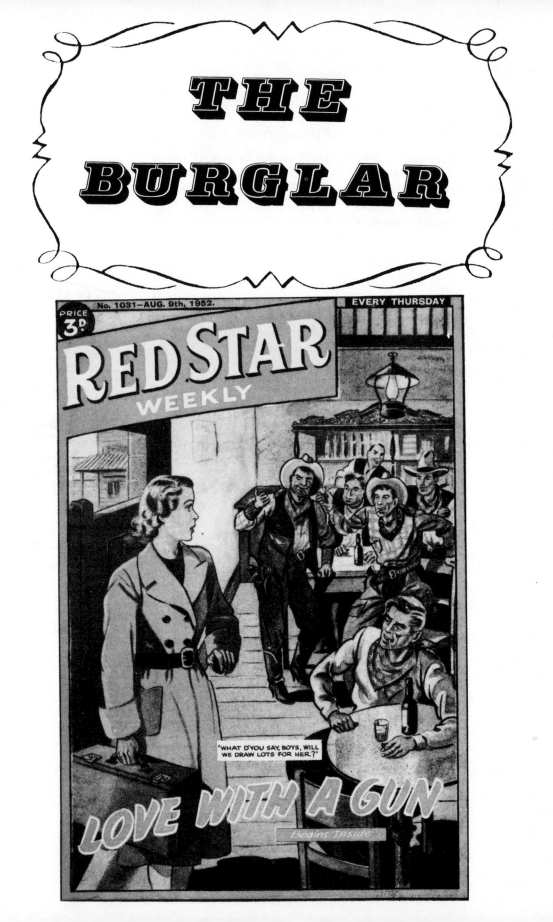

The pub, lunch-time. Pub hubbub, over which:

LANDLORD: (*shouting*) Come on, gents, time please. Time, gentlemen, please. Finish up now, Mr Glum, if you don't mind. I must say, Mr Glum, you seem very pleased with yourself this afternoon.

MR GLUM: More than pleased, Ted. Happy. You are looking at a man whose cup of joy is filled to the brim. Which is more than I can say of this glass. Put another brown in there, will you? The *reason* for my cheerfulness, Ted, is I have pulled off a stroke which will not only benefit me — but my dear son as well. You know my son Ron, don't you?

LANDLORD: Isn't he the one who always asks for a stick of celery and two pickled onions?

MR GLUM: That's him. He's teaching himself bar billiards. Well, what laid the groundwork for the whole scheme was a couple of weeks back. When him and Eth was on the sofa in our front room. And for once — them sofa-strings were not twanging out their usual song ...

Music, and we hark back to the Glums' sitting-room, night.

Eth and Ron are on the sofa.

ETH: Oh, Ron, I heard it again! I'm sure it's somebody moving around upstairs. Please, beloved, just to reassure me, wouldn't you like to just venture up to the landing and see if somebody *has* broken in?

RON: No, Eth.

ETH: But I'm not imagining the noise, Ron. I *keep* hearing it. It's like a — creak.

As she listens fearfully, a slight creaking noise is heard from upstairs.

ETH: There! There it went again.

RON: Oh, Eth, it's probably just the cistern

ETH: Ron, a cistern doesn't make a creak.

RON: Ours does. It makes one right across the bathroom floor. Dad used to belt *me* for it.

ETH: I'm talking about a *noise*-creak. Ron, there's somebody prowling *around* up there. (*Creak*) Listen! I heard it again! Something definitely went creak-creak! ... Oh, Ron, might it be just your woodwork? When this house cools down, does the wood *contract*?

RON: Contract what, Eth?

ETH: Well, you know — in the winter, does the furniture, like, get smaller?

RON: Well, Mum's wardrobe does.

ETH: You sure, Ron?

RON: Oh yes. Dad keeps breaking bits off for the fire.

ETH: Well, if you can assure me that's all it is, I'd feel much better. You really are positive those noises upstairs are just the woodwork contracting?

Before Ron can answer, there are two loud thumps and a crash of china from upstairs.

RON: ... Yes, Eth.

ETH: Ron Glum, that was no woodwork! There's a *burglar* in this house! He's moving around up in — (*Voice drops to horrified whisper*) Ron! Ron, look!

Ron follows the direction of her pointing finger. The door knob is slowly turning.

RON: (*little terror noise*) Awk!

He runs to sideboard — tries to pull out the top drawer.

ETH: Ron, no! You *can't*! You're too *tall* to get in there! Ron, don't desert me. (*Pointing at door*) Oogh!

The door slowly opens — to reveal Mr Glum standing there.

MR GLUM: 'Allo, 'allo, 'allo. I didn't knock in case I missed something. Ron, have you no more pride in your home than to hang your soaking wet mac up in the *hall*? It's dripping all over my motor bike. What *you* staring at, Eth ... Is there something untoward?

ETH: (*gasp of relief*) Ooogh, Mr Glum. I've never been so glad to see anyone in my life. Oh, Mr Glum, we've been sitting here and ... ohh. You've no idea the thoughts that have been going through our minds.

MR GLUM: (*chuckle*) I bet I *have*, Eth. I was young myself once.

ETH: Thoughts about *burglars*, Mr Glum. Oh, Ron, what a relief, eh? Turns out it was actually your father all the time.

RON: Yes, Eth. Same as with Santa Claus.

ETH: You see, Mr Glum, I heard these noises upstairs and — soppy me! — I thought it was a burglar. But now I know it was *you* up there —

MR GLUM: Me? I've only just come in the front door.

ETH: Then ... Oh Ron!

RON: Awk!

He dashes for sideboard drawer; Mr Glum slaps his hands away from it.

MR GLUM: Get your hands out of there! I've already *told* you, you don't get that Marilyn Monroe calendar back till I've rubbed the pencil marks off! And, Eth — I'm surprised at *you*! Going in for hysterical imaginings like that. I've always considered you level-*headed*. You're level enough everywhere else.

ETH: Mr Glum, I know it's silly, but I'll swear I heard a burglar upstairs. If you'd just go and have one little look —

MR GLUM: Eth, you can take my word for it — there is no burglar upstairs. So let that be the end of the matter.

From upstairs comes a sudden clattering noise.

ETH: What was that, Mr Glum?

MR GLUM: (*uneasily*) What was what?

ETH: That clatter. Please, Mr Glum, please go and look.

MR GLUM: Once and for all, Eth, there is no —

He's interrupted by another clatter from upstairs.

MR GLUM: There is —

Again, he's interrupted by a clatter from upstairs.

MR GLUM: There —

Once more a clattering upstairs interrupts him.

MR GLUM (*shout*) Will you let me finish what I'm saying! (*Pause; voice down*) There is no burglar upstairs.

Footsteps are heard descending the stairway.

ETH: (*terror*) He's coming down the stairs!

RON: (*terror*) Dad, he's coming down the stairs! Oh Dad … !

They all rush into each other.

MR GLUM: Now don't panic! (*Grabbing them*) Ron, we'll just *hurt* each other if you try and get behind me at the same time I'm trying to get behind Eth. Just keep calm! Now, Ron — (*There's a knock on the door*) Wossat?

ETH: He wants to come *in*! Don't open it, Mr Glum, don't open it!

Another knock on door.

MR GLUM: Ron, give me over that poker!

RON: (*whisper*) Right.

He hands it to him.

MR GLUM: (*shout of agony*) Aaagh! Not the hot end! Oogh, my hand! (*Calls*) I surrender! I surrender! Come in, mate, take what you want. Have the lot!

The burglar enters. He's a small, meek man, carrying a sack, torch and jemmy.

BURGLAR: (*timidly*) What-ho!

ETH: (*horror*) Oh, Ron — he'll murder us! Ron, for heaven's sake, *say* something to him!

RON: … Hallo, Uncle Charlie.

BURGLAR: Hallo, Ron. (*Nods greeting to Mr Glum*) I'm sorry to break in on you like this.

ETH: Ron, I don't understand. You mean this is — your Uncle Charlie?

RON: Yes, Eth.

ETH: But he's a — burglar.

MR GLUM: Oh, that's all right, Eth. He's not a very good one. (*patiently*) Charlie, whatever you doing burgling *us*?

BURGLAR: (*apologetic*) I didn't *recognize* the house till I got inside.

MR GLUM: Oh, Charlie … Charlie! You've simply got to thieve yourself a new pair of glasses.

BURGLAR: I am most terribly sorry. I just noticed the open window and the drainpipe and, well — before I knew it, I was inside and moving around noiselessly.

MR GLUM: Noiselessly? All that thudding and crashing?

BURGLAR: (*shamefaced*) My torch battery gave out.

ETH: A professional burglar! Mr Glum, you told me Ron's Uncle Charlie was a *biologist*.

MR GLUM: All I said was, he studies cell structures. And there's no need to keep cringing away like that — he's not one of those burglars you *read* about.

ETH: How do you mean?

RON: He's always getting caught.

MR GLUM: (*sharply*) Ron, don't be needlessly *cruel*. (*Mouths a remonstrative 'not in front of him' to Ron*) What I meant, Eth, is that there's nothing vicious or anti-social about Uncle Charlie's burgling. Right?

BURGLAR: (*nods*) In fact, Miss, I find many families welcome being done by a small friendly burglar like myself.

ETH: Welcome?

BURGLAR: It's the insurance, you see. Whatever little I steal from them, they go and tell the insurance company it was much more. So after the insurance company's paid them, they're better off for my visit.

MR GLUM See, Eth? A kind of Robin Hood of the Prudential. In fact … come to think of it — (*he gnaws his moustache*) — Charlie, let me ask you something. It's just a hypertheatrical question but — well, suppose you *had* stolen something here tonight … something like — lessee. What's my most *valuable* possession?

RON: (*shy*) Me, Dad?

MR GLUM: I was thinking about my watch! Something that *works*. What I'm getting at, Charlie, is — if you *had* stolen my watch, would there be anything to stop *me* making out to the insurance company you'd nicked some *other* valuable things as well?

BURGLAR: Nothing. And they'd pay you out for the whole lot.

MR GLUM: Would they now? (*Takes the jemmy from him, weighs it in his hand*) Mm. This should do it nicely.

BURGLAR: Do what?

MR GLUM: The locked drawer in what's left of Mrs Glum's wardrobe.

24

You'll find the watch stuffed at the back. (*Hands jemmy back to him — burglar refuses to accept it*)

BURGLAR: Oh no, I couldn't do *that*. I couldn't.

MR GLUM: Couldn't do what?

BURGLAR: Half-inch from *family*. Nicking from strangers is one thing, but nicking from my own relations — that's *stealing*.

ETH: It's also defrauding an insurance company, Mr Glum. I could never be party to —

MR GLUM: To a nice weekend in *Brighton*, Eth? The three of us? All expenses paid by Eagle Union Accident and Theft?

ETH: Oh ... (*weakly*) Well —

MR GLUM: And all that's keeping us from it is a little co-operation from Uncle Charlie.

BURGLAR: I'd like to, honest. But — I'd never be able to live with myself.

MR GLUM: Well, live with somebody else! Charlie — your favourite nephew? (*Burglar gestures helplessly*) Is that your final word?

BURGLAR: Don't think it doesn't wound *me* as well. In fact, I — I'd prefer to go now. If you'll just let me have my jemmy back, I can prise my own way out. Nice to have met you, Miss.

He leaves.

ETH: Well, Mr Glum, that was a nice thought on your part, but —

MR GLUM: But nothing! Do you think I give up that easy? Ron'll tell you. When I'm on to something I want badly, well — I'm like a bulldog, aren't I?

RON: You mean — the slobbering?

MR GLUM: I mean my stick-at-it-ativeness. Look, why do we even *need* Uncle Charlie? We've *got* all the marks of a burglary. Footprints on the drainpipe, jemmy-marks on the door ... that's quite enough. Ron, dial the police.

RON: (*going to phone*) Right ho, Dad ... (*Dials*) ... Nine ... nine ... (*Pause*) ... er ...

ETH: Nine, beloved.

RON: Oh! *Nine*.

MR GLUM: (*takes phone*) Let me do the talking.

As he composes his face, music — and we return to the pub, night.

LANDLORD: Well, you certainly got nerve, Mr Glum, I'll say that. Taking a bit of a *chance* though, weren't you?

MR GLUM: To make money, Ted, you got to take chances. As they say in the City, 'If you want to accumulate you got to expectorate'. Anyway, after the rozzers had bin, I posted off my claim and, ten days later, along comes this insurance fellow, what they call an 'assessor'. I can only tell you, Ted — it was a good job I'd made sure there was no article on that claim form likely to arouse undue suspicion ...

Music, and we are back in the Glums' sitting-room, daytime.

The assessor is sitting at the table, studying Mr Glum's claim form.

ASSESSOR: Now, Mr Glum — this next article you've put down as stolen. The one you describe as 'the wife's diamond tararra' ...

Mr Glum is pacing, puffing a small cigar — a man distraught.

MR GLUM: (*broken-hearted*) I could kill the swine wot whipped that! Not just because it cost thirty-seven pound ten. That fact is of *immaterial*. It's the sentimental value, Mr Palmer. My beloved wife *loved* that tarrarra, didn't she, Eth?

ETH: There, Mr Glum, don't upset yourself.

MR GLUM: Never once did she go to the chip shop without having it on her wrist!

ASSESSOR: On her —? Mr Glum — a tiara is worn on the head.

MR GLUM: (*caught out*) Is it? (*Recovering*) Well, of course it is *usually*. But my beloved wife is one of those ladies cursed with a very small head but very fat wrists.

ASSESSOR: (*unconvinced*) Indeed. Let's go on to this item then. 'Twenty-five pounds for son Ron's camel hair overcoat'.

ETH: Mr Glum, you can't say that Ron's ever had a ... oogh!

Mr Glum has stubbed his cigar down on her hand.

MR GLUM: Oh, I'm sorry, Eth. Just stubbed it there from force of habit. I'm *lost* since that rotten thieving hound took my favourite ashtray. Alabaster.

RON: Now, Dad — name-calling won't help.

ASSESSOR: I was just wondering whether you have a receipt for that coat.

MR GLUM: That was where the thief was so wicked. Not only did he steal those well-beloved chattels listed on the list you have there — Eth's mink wrap, Ron's silk-lined opera cloak — my collection of Louis Quins sniff-boxes ... but he also stole the *receipts* for 'em! Took 'em out my escritoire.

RON: Oh, Dad, I've *told* you not to leave your escritoire hanging over the chair.

MR GLUM: (*sotto*) Stay out of it! 'Escritoire' is French for safe.

RON: 'Safe'?

ASSESSOR: I'll be frank, Mr Glum. You've given the missing items a total valuation of £825 — but as you cannot furnish one receipt, I don't think we can pay out that amount.

MR GLUM: I see. Well, what are you prepared to *go* to, Mr Palmer?

ASSESSOR: What are *you* prepared to go to, Mr Glum?

RON: Brighton.

MR GLUM: (*sotto*) Will you leave the negotiations to me! (*Up*) I'll tell you what I'm willing to do, Mr Palmer. Knock off the odd twenty-five pounds and make it the round eight hundred.

ASSESSOR: Well, I'll tell you what *I'm* willing to do. Knock off the round eight hundred pounds and make it the odd twenty-five.

MR GLUM: Done!

ASSESSOR: Yes, we thought you might agree to that. In fact, we were so confident — (*brings out envelope from pocket, hands it to Mr Glum*)

MR GLUM: Mr Palmer, you have restored my faith in human nature. Ron, show the gentleman out.

RON: It's through here, Mr Palmer.

Ron leaves with the assessor.

ETH: Mr Glum, you actually managed to do it.

Mr Glum tears open envelope. Peers inside.

MR GLUM: (*gleefully*) And *cash*, too! (*Putting envelope in vase on mantelpiece*) Nice man, wasn't he? I so much *prefer* doing business with persons of education and breeding. They're such narnas.

Ron returns.

RON: (*anxious*) Dad, did he suspect anything? Do you think we'll get away with it?

MR GLUM: (*holding up vase*) We've *got* away with it! (*Puts vase back on mantelpiece*) We're completely out of danger.

RON: (*his face lighting up*) Oh, Eth — we're escritoire!

Music, and we return to the pub, lunch-time.

LANDLORD: So you're now off for that week-end in Brighton then?

MR GLUM: Soon as Eth's helped Ron select a new bucket and spade. Then they'll pick me up here, we'll go home to collect the suitcases and the lolly — then heigh-ho for the briny.

Ron and Eth enter, Ron with bucket and spade.

ETH: Mr Glum, come on or we'll miss the train. Ooh, you'll never guess who we ran into.

RON: Uncle Charlie!

MR GLUM: Don't mention him to me. From now on Uncle Charlie's name is anenema in my household.

ETH: He did seem shamefaced. In fact, he scribbled out this note to give you.

She hands it to him.

MR GLUM: It better be an apology. (*Reads*) 'I've had it preying on my mind so much about not helping you the other night, this evening I slipped back into your house and done a sort of nominal job. Good luck with the insurance on it.' (*Laugh*) Cor — talk about too little and too late, eh? Well, he won't get round me that —

ETH: Isn't that a PS there, Mr Glum?

MR GLUM: Oh yes. (*Reads*) 'PS. Not wishing to deprive you of anything really valuable, I left the watch you suggested and just took that old vase on the mantelpiece.'

ETH: That old … Mr Glum!

RON: Dad, he's got — !

MR GLUM: I've been burgled! … Get the Yard! Get Interpol!

Playout music and BLACKOUT.

The Deed Poll

The pub, night. Pub hubbub, over which:

LANDLORD: *(shouting)* Last drinks, please. Drink up, please. Come on, Mr Glum, time to leave. No, it's no good your looking at me all pathetic. I will not lend you that money.

MR GLUM: A mere three guineas, Ted. What is three guineas to a man of your ilk and substance? Ted, I'm asking you as a — oh, what's the use! Like everybody else in this selfish world, you're just not interested in *other* people's troubles.

LANDLORD: I've got troubles of my own, Mr —

MR GLUM: I'm not interested in them! It's my *son* I'm worrying about. My Ron. Unless I can get hold of three guineas for solicitors' fees, that boy's whole *career* could be in joppardy. He faces a future as empty as this glass you're so steadily ignoring.

LANDLORD: Well, if putting another brown in there would —

MR GLUM: It would at least be a *gesture*, wouldn't it? And, while you're at it, put another gesture in *this* one. What's *happened*, you see, Ted, is — well, it all took place yesterday. Eth — she's his fiancée, y'know — well, she was round our place and she couldn't help noticing Ron's face. He had that sort of pathetic, discarded look, like a used Kleenex. Well, of course, she twigged right away —

Music, and we hark back to the Glums' sitting-room, afternoon.

Ron and Eth are on the sofa.

ETH: Oh, Ron, I know what's caused your low spirits, beloved. It's because you failed to get that job in advertising. Right?

RON: Yes, Eth.

ETH: Such a shame. Exactly what position in the advertising agency was it you had your heart on, Ron?

RON: Sandwich-board man.

ETH: Well, quite honestly, Ron, I don't think a sandwich-board man is that desirable an appointment, anyway.

RON: Perhaps not, Eth. But at least it would have kept me off the streets.

ETH: But you mustn't let that reverse get you *down*, beloved. You're behaving as if it's somehow *your* fault you've been out of work for seven years. Ron, no one can say you haven't *tried* to find employment. How many jobs have you gone after in that seven years?

RON: Oh, it's so many I've lost track, Eth. Must be nearly four.

ETH: I just can't understand why you're so consistently turned down. Obviously, there's something that's putting employers off you — but what? Look, Ron when you go up for an interview, what exactly do you *say* to them?

RON: Nothing they could take offence at, Eth. Just — 'Good afternoon, my name's Ron Glum, good afternoon.'

ETH: (*repeats thoughtfully*) 'Good afternoon, my name's Ron ...' Why do you add that second 'good afternoon'?

RON: Well, I'm generally on my way out by then.

ETH: But why's *that*, Ron? Why should people make up their minds so *quickly* not to — wait a minute! Of course! That's *it*! Ron, suddenly the solution has hit me in the eye.

RON: I've had that happen mending a bicycle-tyre.

ETH: Not that sort of solution. The answer! Why employers are put off! Ron, it's your *name*! 'Ron Glum'. Beloved, I bet if you changed your name, you'd change your whole prospects.

RON: Changed my *name*?

ETH: Look, beloved, *think* about the name 'Ron Glum'. Honestly, now — is it the sort of name that inspires *confidence*? The sort of name that, well — opens *doors*?

RON: I don't know, Eth. (*Tries it*) 'Ron Glum', 'Ron Glum'.

Door opens, Mr Glum enters.

MR GLUM: Hallo, hallo, hallo.

RON: (*gesture that says 'It opened that one'*)

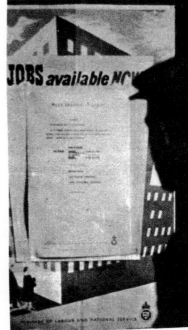

MR GLUM: Sorry to interrupt, but — Ron, have you seen the sink plunger? Your mother needs it to mash the potatoes. What *you* looking so excited about, Eth?

ETH: Mr Glum, I think I've worked out what's kept Ron out of work so long.

MR GLUM: If you're talking about that one with the sandwich-boards, he'd never have been able to carry 'em anyway — not with his sort of shape. Look at him. About as much breadth of shoulder as a banana.

ETH: That *wasn't* why he failed to attain the post, Mr Glum. What's been holding Ron back all these years is his name. Mr Glum, he's got to *change* it.

MR GLUM: Change his — oh, don't talk so wet, Eth. It took him till he was fifteen to remember the one he's got. Change his name? What's the purpose?

ETH: Look, Mr Glum, just imagine you're that sandwich-board employer and there's *two* people come for the job. One says 'My name's Ron Glum,' the other says 'My name's' — oh — 'Ludovic Kennedy.' Now, Mr Glum — just on names alone, which one would you *choose*?

MR GLUM: (*doubtfully*) Well ...

RON: (*getting up and leaving*) Good afternoon.

ETH: (*pulling him back*) No, Ron, we were only supposing. But see what happened, Mr Glum? He knew at the *outsit* he didn't have a chance. It really is a *handicap* being called 'Ron Glum'. Can't you appreciate that?

MR GLUM: Well, in a *way*, I suppose, but — but, Eth, changing the name doesn't in any way change *him*. I mean, look at Uncle Charlie. *He's* been

There'll Be No Holiday For The Kershaw Family

Back To The Dole In 1952

by JAMES CAMERON

Fred Kershaw, like thousands more, clings to a cotton industry in which there is no
work for him. Abruptly, last year's cash and confidence have given way to worry

FROM the moors beyond Oldham in east Lancashire, on what passes there for a clear day, it is possible to count a hundred tall chimneys rising from the brick jungle below. They stand out among the huddled houses and bulky mills, breathing forth their contribution to the grey film that settles over wall and window, street and floor.

It is a view to make a painter flinch; cotton-mill chimneys are charmless things. But if they are there, they should smoke; it is when the smoke stops that the textile town is truly sombre. It is stopping now.

What is this story about a cotton slump? Is there really a slump? Is it a temporary thing, or is Lancashire back to the dismal thirties?

Until a month or two ago nobody outside the cotton towns seemed to know anything about this sudden island of depression in the national sea of full employment. Not until the north-country M.P.s abruptly startled Parliament into a twenty-hour debate did the whole nation realize that the traditional staple barometer-trade of the North was flopping again.

Postwar prosperity had been undermined in the dark by extravagant world conditions, and this year the roof fell in. At Christmas there were solid wages and good bonuses, now there is short time and no time. Six months ago there was confidence and cash, now there is doubt and indeed fear. This year—ironically the first year with a legal fortnight's holiday-with-pay—the word "holiday" has a desperate sound. Is it really back to the dole?

A Lifetime Of Spinning

I decided to ask somebody; Fred Kershaw, for instance. At thirty-eight, he has been a spinner all his working life, which is about twenty-three years. Now he does not spin, and the working life has stopped. He is not "typical"—few men ever are—being at the same time greatly worse and somewhat better off than many of his unemployed colleagues. He is one of the 150,000-odd operatives in the

English cotton-textile trade who have been affected. It *is* back to the dole for him. The holiday at Blackpool is out this year.

Kershaw lives in Oldham, which has a registered working population of 38,000. More than 10,000 of these workers are directly employed in the spinning industry. Six months ago you could have put practically the whole of Oldham's unemployed into a moderate-sized room. Now, in this town alone, more than 7,000 people are wholly or almost wholly out of work, in circumstances where being "partly employed" can mean one week's work in nine.

The reasons for this and its implications are complex and alarming. Nevertheless, through the eyes of Fred Kershaw a position that is grim has a remarkable simplicity.

Two Weeks' Work In Eleven

He is "wholly unemployed," and it was not so easy, curiously, to find such a man, for the technical term means that the job must have completely vanished. Thousands are working one week and "playing," in the bitter Lancashire phrase, for many more. Before Fred Kershaw's work stopped indefinitely he was employed two weeks out of eleven.

With his abundant family he lives in a windy little house, like a farm cottage, on a ridge just above the town, with a vaporous aspect of Oldham below and the moors of Yorkshire ahead. He has a wife, seven children, and a goat. His circumstances are perhaps slightly exceptional—in the multitude of his family and also in the position of his home, which is probably as near to a pastoral scene as that relentless county produces, making possible the presence of Nancy the goat, which is important.

Consider the simple economics of the situation. Fred Kershaw is, or was, in the top grade of spinners, and brought home something more than ten pounds a week—by no means too much, one would say, for a family of nine. Now his income is: the dole, £1 12s. 6d., plus £1 1s. 6d. for a dependent wife, plus 10s. 6d. for the first child and 2s. 6d. each for the six

Cotton paid Kershaw £10 a week. Now, dole and allowances make £6 14s.—for a family of nine

all *sorts* of names in his time. Lord Selwyn Harcourt, Major Winthrop Audley, VC, Anastasia — (*shakes his head*) — Forlorn ruddy hope *that* was! What else? The Bishop of North Auckland — er ... what's the one he's living under the moment, Ron?

RON: Seven-eight-four-one-four.

MR GLUM: Yes, but the point is he's still the same Uncle Charlie. I mean *inside*. Which is where he happens to be now. Do you see what I'm getting at?

ETH: (*heated*) All I see is, by refusing to let Ron change his name, you're simply keeping him from employment for the whole rest of his life.

MR GLUM: Oh, that's nice to hear, isn't it? You know, Eth, you can be very wounding sometimes. I know you mean well, but you got a tongue on you like a claw. Would I do a thing like that? To my own flesh and bone? Stubborn I may be — but one thing you don't seem to realize. I am a *father*.

RON: Dad, congratulations. Eth, I'm going to have a little —

MR GLUM: Will you belt up! I wish you'd do me the common civility of keeping *out* of it when I'm having a discussion with you. All right, Eth, let's for a moment accept this hypotenuse you have put forward. Suppose we do change his name. May I ask one question — what *to*?

ETH: Well, as long as it's something more *inspiring* than 'Ron Glum'. More — melodious.

MR GLUM: How about ... 'Alf Potts'? Well, don't look down your nose, Eth. I've known some very nice Potts.

ETH: Yes, but if we're going to do it, why not choose some really impressive name? After all, I'm going to be *Mrs* whatever-it-is. Ron, haven't you got a suggestion? What would *you* like to be called?

RON: (*considers*) ... 'Wyatt Earp'.

ETH: Oh, Ron. 'Wyatt' isn't an *English* kind of Christian name.

RON: 'Ron Earp'?

ETH: No.

RON: 'Anastasia Earp'?

MR GLUM: May *I* make a suggestion now, Ron?

RON: Yes, Dad.

MR GLUM: *Shut* Earp!

ETH: Mr Glum, let's keep our tempers. Know what I've always liked? Surnames that end with 'son'? You know — 'Davidson', 'Wilkinson' ...

RON: '*Earp*son'?

MR GLUM: Oh, for heaven's sake, it can't be *that* difficult to find a name that 'opens doors'. Here — (*chuckle*) — how about 'Nobbs'? Oh, don't go all sniffy again, Eth. That was the kind of Cockney humour that got us through the Blitz.

ETH: But does it help when you're trying to *concentrate*? Question is, what sort of name would *suit* Ron? You know how sometimes you can look at a person and say, 'He is definitely a "David".' Or somebody else could only be a 'Harold'. Now, looking at Ron, what would you say he is *a*?

(*They both look at him*)

MR GLUM: ... We'd never get it past Somerset House, Eth.

RON: 'Henry Turner'.

ETH: Pardon, Ron?

RON: The name just came to me, Eth. 'Henry Turner'.

ETH: Mmmm ... Let me sort of try it out. 'Henry Turner'. 'Mrs Henry Turner'. 'Henry and Ethel Turner'. 'His Worshipful and Lady Turner' ...

MR GLUM: Leave it at that, Eth. (*Snaps his fingers*) Back to earth.

ETH: I like it, Mr Glum, I like it very much. It's dignified without being overpowering. Oh, well done, Ron!

RON: You should have asked me in the first place.

MR GLUM: All right, no need to show off, Henry. So what's the next step, Eth?

ETH: Well, I think we have to have some kind of official document drawn up by a solicitor.

MR GLUM: (*going to door*) Of which there are several in the High Street. So — (*opens door with a flourish*) — after you, Lady Turner.

As Eth gets up to go with him, music — and the scene changes to a solicitor's office, same afternoon.

The solicitor is at his desk — Mr Glum, Ron and Eth sitting opposite him.

SOLICITOR: Yes, the name by which the procedure is generally known is 'deed poll', a very simple process costing only three guineas and extremely common these days. Only this morning I had another client in to effect a change in surname — a Mr Smellie.

RON: (*eyes light up*) Ooh, Dad — can't I —

MR GLUM: No, you *can't*! We've picked your name!

RON: But if he's finished with it — ?

ETH: We've *decided*, Ron. Oh, isn't it sad? That's probably the last time I'll be calling you 'Ron'.

SOLICITOR: 'Ron' being one of the names you're seeking to alter, I take it. In favour of what?

MR GLUM: In favour of employment. Because this lad's been up the Labour Exchange every day for seven years. I reckon the manager there's seen more of him than he has of his own wife.

SOLICITOR: (*dry chuckle*) I doubt it. He's a bachelor.

ETH: Oh, you're acquainted with the manager of the Labour Exchange then?

SOLICITOR: Old Henry Turner? Oh, yes we've been members of the same —

MR GLUM: Who'd you say? What's his name?

SOLICITOR: Henry Turner.

ETH: (*wail*) Oh, Ron!

On Eth's wail, music — and we go back to the Glums' sitting-room, later.

MR GLUM: (*bitterly*) 'The name just came to me,' he says. You great cloth-headed oaf! If you'd have breezed into that Labour Exchange and announced yourself as Henry Turner, you'd have been lucky to get out of there without having your benefits cut off.

ETH: Oh, don't keep on about it, Mr Glum. Let's keep searching through the phone-books for more *possibilities*. Found anything in the S to Z book, Ron?

RON: How about — how about 'Ken Soso'?

MR GLUM: Ken ... ? That's the *number*. 'Kensington five-oh-five-oh'! Look, we've been three hours on this. Who'd think it'd be so *difficult*? One rotten name ... 'Percival'? ... 'Humphrey'? ... 'Humphrey Percival'? ... *useless*! I hope you realize if we go on much longer with this, we're into drinking time.

RON: (*closing book*) It's all right, Dad, I've got one!

MR GLUM: Yes?

ETH: Yes, Ron?

RON: No, it's gone again.

MR GLUM: Would you Adam-and-Eve it!

RON: Wait a minute, it's coming back.

ETH: Yes?

RON: (*triumph*) 'Stewart Mulholland'.

MR GLUM: 'Stewart Mulholland'? *Sold*! Sold to the gentleman in the hairy cap. (*Rising*) Come on!

As they follow him, music — and we come back to the solicitor's office, later.

SOLICITOR: Well, I'm glad you found another name so quickly. Quite sure you're *happy* with this one?

MR GLUM: Well, I don't know about happy — but you get to the stage where *every* name sounds a bit crackpot.

SOLICITOR: Well, I suppose even a crackpot name is better than the one he's ... (*coughs*) Let's complete the deed then, shall we? If you'll just tell

Bang!

MORE than 100,000 people at Castle Bromwich, **Birmingham**, saw and heard Flying-Officer P. K. Cranston, of Toronto, break the sound barrier in his Sabre jet during yesterday's Battle of Britain display.

Sound barrier was also broken by RCAF pilot Flying-Officer R. Paquette, at **Horsham St. Faith**, Norfolk. And 10,000 heard him.

NO BANG

At **Biggin Hill**, Kent, 120,000 were disappointed because test pilot Neville Duke did not fly faster than sound in his Hunter fighter. The ban came from the Air Ministry.

In a mock fighter-bomber attack on ground troops at **Hendon** RAF Station, a Very light slightly burned a woman and her young niece. They went home after first-aid treatment.

Daily Mirror

TUES JUNE 23 1953

1½d FORWARD WITH THE PEOPLE
No. 15,429

CHRISTIE REVELATIONS

ACCUSED BY MAN WHO WAS HANGED

By HOWARD JOHNSON

SENSATIONAL REVELATIONS ABOUT THE PAST LIFE OF JOHN CHRISTIE WERE MADE LAST NIGHT AT THE END OF THE FIRST DAY OF HIS TRIAL FOR MURDER.

Christie, the jury at London's Old Bailey were told, is a man with a criminal record—he has served three prison sentences for theft, and one for maliciously wounding a woman by striking her on the head with a cricket bat.

dering his wife, Ethel, 54, at No. 10, Rillington-place. He pleaded "Not guilty" in a whisper.

Soon it became clear that the crucial issue before the jury in one of the most sensational murder trials of the century will be the mind of John Christie—WAS HE SANE OR INSANE WHEN HIS WIFE WAS KILLED?

● THE CASE FOR THE DEFENCE is that Christie was legally insane when his wife was killed, Mr. Curtis-Bennett, Q.C. told the jury of nine men and three women. And it was Mr. Curtis-Bennett who first mentioned "other women killed" at No. 10, and was given the right to cross-examine witnesses about them.

● THE CASE FOR THE CROWN is that Christie murdered his wife, that he knew that what he was doing was wrong, and that he lied, deceived and committed forgery to cover it up, said the Attorney-General, Sir Lionel Heald, Q.C.

FULL REPORT BEGINS ON PAGE

I Want His Whole Life Story, Says Counsel

● The convict

More troops for Korea?

BRITAIN, in one of the strongest protest Notes ever sent to an Allied Government, yesterday accused South Korea's President, Syngman Rhee, of treachery. And Sir Winston Churchill, after telling the Commons about the Note, added : " Now we do not know quite what will happen.

IT MIGHT BE THAT REINFORCEMENT WILL BE NEEDED FOR KOREA IN ORDER TO ENFORCE A POLICY OF PEACE AND GOOD FAITH."

'Traitor to the U.N.'

The Note said that Britain had been shocked by Rhee's order freeing thousands of anti-communist North Korean prisoners. It made it quite clear that the British G......

WHAT STALIN THINKS OF A-BOMB, KOREA, WAR AND PEACE

All troops may go by Comet

"PICTORIAL" AIR CORRESPONDENT

A SECRET plan to make all British infantry divisions airborne is being studied by Mr. Churchill while me what name it is you've —(*his phone rings*) Oh, excuse me. (*Into phone*) Hallo? Yes, this is Stewart Mulholland speaking. Certainly I will. By tomorrow? Fine. Goodbye then. (*He puts the receiver down, looks up*) Sorry about that, Mr Glum, I — (*he stares. There is no one there. The office has emptied.*)

Music, and we return to the Glums' sitting-room, later.

ETH: (*wail*) No, Mr Glum, no! Just because you're ratty, I am *not* going to spend the rest of my life as Mrs Smellie.

MR GLUM: Ratty? I'm livid! A vivid livid! That's the second time he's had me looking a complete — (*breaks off; thoughtfully*) — 'Albert Burke'? 'Thomas Burke'? 'Quintin Burke'? ... No, I am *not* going to be set off on that meandering again. We'll settle this now, once and for all. If you can't decide on a name, I shall just *confer* one on you willy-nilly.

RON: Yes, that's a *good* one, I like that, Dad. Willy —

MR GLUM: Not another word! Take that S to Z phone book, Ron. Now open it at random.

RON: Oh, Dad! (*Pointing to another book*) Random's in the L to R book.

MR GLUM: (*helplessly*) Is there such a thing as getting a divorce from a *son*? What I mean is, we'll let *chance* settle the matter. Give me the book here. (*Takes it*) Now where's a —? (*Finds a pin*) Ah! Right ... (*Closes his eyes*) Now, wherever this pin lands — that is *it*! (*Plunges pin down. Eyes still closed*) Tell me who I'm stuck on, Eth?

ETH: (*peers*) 'Fenton Worsley'.

MR GLUM: (*opening eyes*) Could have been worse. Could have been a lot worse. So what we now do is this. Eth, you got that three guineas ready? (*Eth gives it to Mr Glum, who hands it to Ron*) You go along to that solicitor right away and give him this. And you also hand him *this*. (*Mr Glum tears out the page from phone-book — hands it to Ron*) You give him my apologies and you tell him that your new name is the one that's got the little *hole* in it. Understand?

RON: But, Dad —

MR GLUM: (*voice of thunder*) Ron!

RON: ... Good afternoon.

As he dutifully makes for door — music and we change the scene to the pub, night.

Mr Glum and landlord are now the only ones left there.

LANDLORD: But if he's gone off and *changed* his name, Mr Glum, I don't see what you want another three guineas for?

MR GLUM: To change it *back* again.

LANDLORD: Oh, *why*? I think Fenton Worsley's a nice name.

MR GLUM: So do I, Ted. But we're dealing with Ron, you see. And it was only earlier this evening that it came to me like a thunderclap. There's

Outside the stage-door Spike Milligan signs for a few youthful admirers

one thing you have to remember about a piece of paper with a hole in it.

LANDLORD: (*knits brows, then*) Oh, no!

MR GLUM: And when Ron gets here, I'll bet any money — ah!

Ron enters, carrying paper.

RON: Hallo, Dad.

MR GLUM: (*strangely calm*) Hallo, Ron. Did exactly what I told you, did you, son?

RON: Exactly, Dad. Just like you said. (*Hands Mr Glum paper, points proudly to hole*) That's who I am now.

MR GLUM: (*stares at paper. Shows it to Ted*) What did I tell you? (*Reverses paper — points to hole*) Fenton Worsley. (*Turns paper back to side Ron handed him*) And this is my son — (*points; bitterly*) Lee Fu Wong!

Playout music and BLACKOUT.

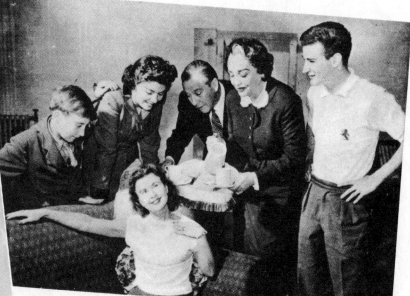

Well, here's a turn up for the book—the Lyon family wait upon Aggie for a change. They know the worth of Molly Weir— and so do millions of viewers

DAVID NIXON

PILFERING

A hunted and desperate woman, Katherine is at the end of her tether.

ONLY ONE WOMAN KNEW

"I'm sorry, Doctor," the Inspector said, "but I have a warrant for your daughter's arrest."

A BAD ONE TO MARRY

All her money was gone. Someone had stolen it! To Katherine it was the last straw.

The pub, night. Pub hubbub, over which:

LANDLORD: (*shouting*) Time, gentlemen, please. All your glasses, please, gentlemen. Drink up, Mr Glum. Here, Mr Glum, I must say — you have the look of a man who has, how shall I say, fulfilled himself.

MR GLUM: Well, I don't know about fulfilling meself, Ted. I've certainly filled meself full. And shall I tell you *why* I have abandoned my customary moderation? 'Cos I have done a good deed. I saw where there was an *injustice* — and, as is my wont, I did my best to readdress it. Because, after all, Ted — if we cannot help our fellow creatures, what are we here for?

LANDLORD: Well, no longer than five minutes I hope, Mr Glum. I've got my licence to —

MR GLUM: Oh, for heaven's sake, Ted — let us not confuse licence with liberty. Because what *I* happened on this week was a *real* liberty. Insert another brown in this receptacle and I'll tell you about it. The victim in question was my son's fiancée — young Eth. Last Monday she was round our house on the sofa. And, Ted, it was obvious to the meanest intelligence — namely, my son Ron — that something was troubling her. She had an expression on her face I can only describe as like a ruptured marshmallow ...

Music, and we hark back to the Glums' sitting-room, night.

Ron and Eth are on the sofa.

ETH: Oh, Ron ... I'm sorry to be such a wet blanket tonight. But I'm so distraught, I just — oh, beloved, this is a time when I need all your love. Ron, bring your dear face close to mine and look at me.

RON: Righty-ho, Eth.

ETH: Right close, Ron. Right *tight* close.

RON: I can't bring it any closer, Eth. Our noses will bash.

ETH: Then hold my cheeks. Ron, my dearest heart, gaze deep in my eyes ... Now, beloved, I want you to answer me something — from your *heart*. Ron — Ron of mine — if I swore to you I *hadn't* done something but everybody else swore I *had* — who would you believe? Me or them?

RON: Them.

ETH: Ron!

RON: All right then, me.

ETH: Ron! It's me they're *saying* things about. You see, Ron, last week there was a shortage in the petty cash. And the manager says it must have been stolen by one of us girls. We've got a pilferer.

RON: How are you going to get her to swallow it?

ETH: A thief, Ron. And you know who the manager's saying it is? *Me*! Thirty-eight girls in the general office. Thirty-eight of them. And out of the whole thirty-eight he picks *me*!

RON: Oh, Eth. Congratulations!

ETH: But he's calling me a *thief*! Me, Ron. (*Edge of tears*) I'm being persecuted for something I swear I haven't done. They're treating me like I'm some horrible crim — criminal. Oh, Ron — (*sobs*).

RON: No, don't cry. Eth ... please don't cry. It makes all your massacre run. Please stop, Eth. Your face'll taste all *nasty*. Please Eth ...

ETH: (*wails*)

Door opens, Mr Glum enters, crosses to sideboard.

MR GLUM: Hallo, hallo, hallo. I won't interrupt you two if you're enjoying yourselves. (*Goes to saucepan on sideboard*) Just seeing if there's a dumpling left in this stew. (*Lifts one out*) Mrs Glum's out in the garden and I want to attract her attention. (*Notices Eth*) 'Ere, Ron, what's *she* so upset about?

RON: She hasn't done something, Dad.

ETH: But everybody's saying I *have* done it, Mr Glum. I *haven't*, I swear I —

MR GLUM: Now, just calm down, Eth. Stop that crying this instance. You're just making your face look a slice of brawn. Come on now, give over, there's a good girl. Ron, got a hankie?

RON: (*extracting one*) Yes, Dad.

MR GLUM: Then *use* it! (*Ron wipes his nose*) Now, Eth, what is all this 'have-done-it, ain't-done-it' business?

ETH: Well, I — I suppose it would help to tell you about it. I've been feeling like I've got to unburden my secret or *bust*!

MR GLUM: Well, the former would seem a more attractive alternative. What's up then, girl?

ETH: Mr Glum, life at the office has become unbearable. I'm under suspicion of stealing from the petty cash. So everybody's treating me like a leper. If you knew — the whispering, the pointing ... I can't *take* much more of it.

RON: How much have you taken so far?

ETH: I haven't taken *any*! I'm innocent! Would I take what didn't belong to me, would I stoop to —

MR GLUM: All right, all right. Let's not have hysterics. Let's talk it over like rational human beings. Now, first things first. Can you tell me exactly what has been half-inched and its approximate floggable value?

ETH: A sheet of Health Insurance stamps. Amounting in value to eight pound eleven shillings. They were kept locked up in the petty cash box.

MR GLUM: I see. The petty cash box. Well now, what sort of people have access?

RON: Lumberjacks, Dad. They use 'em for —

MR GLUM: Not axes! *Access*! In other words, Eth, who's got *keys* to the petty cash box?

ETH: Well, that's *it*. Only me.

MR GLUM: Oh. Oh, dear.

ETH: That's why I'm under suspicion.

MR GLUM: Yes, I can see that. Very understandable, too. Mmm. Well, looks pretty black, doesn't it, Ron?

RON: Certainly does, Dad. I wouldn't be surprised if we didn't have some rain.

MR GLUM: I'm referring to 'The case against Madame Eth'. (*To Eth*) After all, if you are the only one possessing a key —

ETH: But, Mr Glum, as I said to the manager — that key is only kept in my desk-drawer. Almost anyone could have borrowed it and put it back after. Couldn't they?

MR GLUM: (*sceptically*) They *could*, yes.

ETH: Mr Glum, I can tell by your tone what's going through your mind. You don't believe me. And you're having second thoughts about inviting into your family someone who's been branded — 'Thief'.

MR GLUM: So that's what you think, is it? Well, I don't know what kind of narrow-minded bigot you take me for — but suppose I tell you I would *welcome* having a thief in the Glum family?

ETH: Welcome?

MR GLUM: Certainly. Be company for Uncle Charlie. You haven't met him yet, Eth, but I can assure you, in his day, Ron's Uncle Charlie was as sticky-fingered a larceny expert as ever plagued E Division. I mean, you have to take your hat off to a man who can walk out of the Ideal Home Exhibition concealing a *loft-ladder*! Oh, a right villain, old Charlie was. Bent as a crankshaft. But now he's reformed and taken up honest employment — well, I'm sure he'd *welcome* talking over tricks of the trade with a kindred spirit.

ETH: Kindred —! Mr Glum, once for all, I *didn't* take those health stamps.

MR GLUM: (*disbelievingly*) I know, I know. But couldn't you have stole 'em without *realizing* it? How do you know you're not one of those — what do they call them? — one of those maniacs who go round *klepting* things? What's the word, Ron?

RON: Hypochondriac?

MR GLUM: Something like that. Anyway, Eth, the truth will all come out when they get the police in.

ETH: But they *won't* get the police in.

MR GLUM: Why not?

ETH: Oh, if you or Ron had ever *had* regular employment, you'd know how these firms do it. They don't like fuss. All that'll happen is, I'll be quietly sacked — with no references. So I'll never be able to get myself a job anywhere ever again!

RON: (comfortingly) Well, there you are, Eth. Everything turns out for the best.

ETH: But I don't *want* to be forever called a thief when I know I'm not. Isn't there *anyone* who can help me? Mr Glum, couldn't I — couldn't I hire private detectives?

MR GLUM: Ooh, I dunno. They cost quite a bit of money.

RON: And you've only got eight pound eleven shillings.

ETH: I *haven't*, Ron! For the umpteenth time, I — oh, what's the use!

MR GLUM: Eth, I know how you feel but — well, I think there's something I should tell you that may be of some comfort. A story I — I've never told no one before. Forty years ago, someone *else* was unjustly accused of a crime. Someone very much your age, Eth — but a young ... *feller*. And he, too, was charged with stealing some money from the firm's till. He protested his innocence but — to no avail. They gave him six months. A young man — in the prime of youth — sent to prison for six months for a theft that was committed by somebody else.

ETH: (timidly) Mr Glum ... was that — *you*?

MR GLUM: (sigh) Yes, Eth, that was me. Can't remember the name of the young feller who went to prison ... But you see the moral?

ETH: (blazing) No, I *don't*! Oh, it's — it's like banging your head against a vicious circle. (Pleading) Mr Glum, seeing you've *had* the experience — couldn't *you* come to my office and help clear me?

MR GLUM: I'd like to, Eth, but — where would we even start? We've got nothing to go on.

RON: We could go on my bike, Dad.

MR GLUM: No, what I mean is, they wouldn't even let someone like me in. It's only policemen who could — (long pause) — Policemen ...?

As Mr Glum gazes at Ron speculatively, music — and the scene changes to the manager's office, Eth's firm, the following day.

MANAGER: (dictating) 'And we can confirm delivery on the fifteenth inst. Assuring you of our best attention, etc.' Got that?

ETH: Yes, Mr Hopkins.

MANAGER: Well, when you've finished typing that, Ethel, there's a rather unpleasant personal matter I wish to see you about.

ETH: (stifling a sob) Yes, Mr Hopkins.

Knock on door — door opens. Mr Glum and Ron are standing there in none too well-fitting bowler hats, raincoats and stout boots.

MR GLUM: All right, Mr Hopkins. We're the filth. I'm Inspector Fagin of New Scotland Yard and this is my assistant, Dixon of Golders Green. All right, Dixon, spread out round the room. Dixon, I'm talking to you.

RON: I can't hear you, Dad.

Inside The Joy Factory

Stars taking coffee with chorus girls; boot-blacks at script talks; music in the air—Connery Chappell reports on the M-G-M lot

THIS WAY TO HOLLYWOOD
by THE EDITOR

One of the Joy Factory's latest finds—Denise Darcel, who's featured in the Glenn Ford film, *Young Man in a Hurry*

IN Hollywood everyone is too busy to think of the future. Perhaps that is why so few of the city's buildings look as though they have been made to last.

Sunshine, palm trees and white plaster finishing. Neon signs over plyboard; hot-dog stands and "motels" in search of some architecture. . . . In all this the Joy Factory, Metro-Goldwyn-Mayer's studios, is a solid, almost grim-looking exception.

It shares with the oil derricks the distinction of being the chief item in Culver City, one of the many dormitories of Los Angeles. The district looks exactly like the rest of the sprawling town around it; the same slap-happy streets with their shiny drug ... the same boom-town air; makes films of a serious nature, but none more successful.

The studio itself : . ... place ...

of her star salary. You look around—and count "names," ch...

City is talking about. And what Culver says today th...

MR GLUM: I told you to get a smaller bowler hat! Hoick it up and shove a wedge in.

MANAGER: Inspector, what's this about?

MR GLUM: Tell him, Dixon.

RON: (*a painfully acquired lesson*) On information received, we are making enquiries regarding some property which has been reported pilched.

MANAGER: Pilched?

MR GLUM: (*hastily*) It's a criminological term. Halfway between filched and pilfered.

MANAGER: I'm afraid I don't understand.

RON: It's about those stamps Eth pinched.

ETH: But I didn't pi —

MR GLUM: All right, all right, your evidence will be taken in due course, Miss.

MANAGER: Look here, this intrusion is most extraordinary. May I see your authority?

MR GLUM: (*hands him document; almost immediately takes it back*) There we are. Now as to the matter in question —

MANAGER: (*retrieving it*) Just a minute. You didn't give me time to read it. But this isn't a warrant. This is a summons made out against a ... a Mr Glum. For using abusive language outside the Mission Hall.

MR GLUM: That's right. I'm on me way to deliver it. Now do you believe I'm a copper?

MANAGER: Well, I suppose so. But look here, Inspector, there's absolutely no need for you to intrude in this matter of the Health Stamps. We know that this girl here is the culprit and we shall take our own punitive measures.

ETH: No. Don't let them.

MR GLUM: It's all right, Miss. You realize, Mr Hopkins, that by making false accusations you are liable to a charge of inflammation of the character?

MANAGER: *False* accusations?

MR GLUM: I'll show you the guilty party. Sergeant Dixon —

RON: Yes, Dad?

MR GLUM: Get your finger out that pencil-sharpener and open the window. Mr Hopkins — what do you see in that guttering?

MANAGER: A bird's nest.

MR GLUM: Right. Now, if I can just reach into it — ah, as I thought. (*Exhibits hand*) ... What's this, Mr Hopkins?

MANAGER: A Health Stamp!

MR GLUM: Exactly. And how do you think that stamp got *in* the bird's nest?

RON: You had it in your hand before you — (*Mr Glum's foot comes down on his*) Oogh!

MR GLUM: One more interruption from you, Dixon, and you'll find something else jammed into that pencil-sharpener! There's your culprit, Mr Hopkins — a common or garden *jackdaw*.

MANAGER: I don't understand.

MR GLUM: Jackdaws are famous for flying in windows and pinching bright-coloured objects for lining the nest. Quite obviously that's what your jackdaw did with your Health Stamps while the petty cash box was open.

MANAGER: How absolutely extraordinary! The only thing that puzzles me is — the occupant of *that* nest is a *sparrow*.

MR GLUM: Eh? Oh, well, then we are dealing with no ordinary jackdaw. Not only is he an inveterate thief, but in addition — a master of disguise.

MANAGER: Well, I'll be ... Ethel, I owe you a heartfelt apology. I do hope that a small increase in salary may compensate. As for you, Inspector —

MR GLUM: I know what you're going to say, sir. And though we're not generally allowed to drink on duty, seeing as this is a special occasion ...

MANAGER: Oh! That wasn't really what I was going to — but still. (*Going off*) I'll go and get the bottle and glasses.

MR GLUM: There you are, Eth. 'Inspector Glum Does It Again'.

ETH: That was wonderful, Mr Glum! But did you work out that whole jackdaw idea before you left home?

MR GLUM: No, Eth, I did not. It was only when I stepped into the director's lift to come up here that the entire thing suddenly became crystal-clear. A few seconds' swift discussion and the scheme was concocted.

ETH: But why should coming up in the lift have given it to you?

MR GLUM: Eth, you never use the director's lift, do you?

ETH: Oh no, Mr Glum.

MR GLUM: Then you won't have met the lift-man. Tell her, Ron.

RON: ... It's my Uncle Charlie!

Playout music and BLACKOUT.

The pub, night. Pub hubbub, over which:

LANDLORD: (*shouting*) Time, gentlemen, please. All your glasses, please. Come on, Mr Glum, what's up with you? All night you been sitting there looking thoughtful.

MR GLUM: Yes, I 'ave been, Ted. *Very* retrospective, I bin. And you know what set me off? It was catching sight of that pork pie.

LANDLORD: This one?

MR GLUM: Ass it. Made me remember something *else* that was fresh seven years ago. Namely, Ted, my son Ron's engagement to Eth. You know my son, Ron, don't you?

LANDLORD: Ron ... Ron ... I seem to remember him coming in here, vaguely.

MR GLUM: Yes, that's how he comes in everywhere. But it was exactly seven years ago tonight, he suddenly sprung it on me he'd got himself engaged. Ted — I was aghasted! I'd had no *idea*, you see. *I* thought he'd been depleting his excess energy on bubble gum. However, that night — I'll never forget it! — he'd taken himself off to the pictures, and Ted — hours and *hours* after the cinema'd *closed* — he's not home yet! The state I was in! My mind was churning. *Churning ... !*

Music, and we hark back to the Glums' sitting-room, night.

Mr Glum pacing up and down, worried.

MR GLUM: Where can he *be* till this time of night? Where can —

The clock on the mantelpiece strikes two.

MR GLUM: Gawd! (*Calls*) Mother!

MOTHER'S VOICE FROM UPSTAIRS: (*unintelligible coarse snarling*)

MR GLUM: (*calls*) The mantelpiece clock's just struck *two*! You know what that means? It's twenty past *three*!! And our baby Ron's not back yet! (*Resumes pacing; to himself*) He's never been out this late. (*Dreadful thought*) Perhaps he's had an accident on his bike ... Oh *no*! I *told* him to buy a *proper* skid-lid. What he's using, just keeps slipping down over his *eyes*. And if the *handle* catches on anything — ! (*Anguished, clasps his hands together, casts eyes upwards*) Please — *please* let my baby boy walk through that door safe and unharmed ... I'll bash his head in. Oh, I can't just stay here and — (*He goes to door, shouts upstairs*) I'm going to the front gate and see if I can see him coming!

MOTHER'S VOICE FROM UPSTAIRS: (*unintelligible snarling — on an interrogative note*)

MR GLUM: (*calls*) When I've *found* him, that's when I'll be up! (*To himself*) Cor! She has to choose *tonight* to start reading Lady Chatterley ... !

He exits through door to front hall. As he disappears, there is a moment's pause — then Ron and Eth enter from the opposite door; both in a rosy haze.

ETH: Oh, Ron ...

RON: Oh, Eth ...

They twine

RON: It was very nice of you to see me home.

ETH: I just couldn't bear parting, Ron. But why did we come in the *back* way?

RON: (*softly*) 'Cos the door's narrower.

ETH: I don't see what that's got to do with it.

RON: (*shy*) It means you've got to squeeze past me to get in.

ETH: (*casts her eyes down blushingly*)

RON: I like it, Eth.

ETH: (*tenderly*) Oh, Ron! (*Nuzzles him*)

RON: ... Eth —

ETH: Yes?

RON: Let's go out and come in again.

ETH: No, Ron dearest, no use torturing ourselves. Let's just — sit and talk. (*They sit on the sofa*) Oh, Ron ...

RON: Yes, Eth?

ETH: You did *mean* those three little words you whispered to me in the cinema, didn't you?

RON: 'Course I did, Eth ... I *had* seen it.

ETH: Not regarding the film, Ron. I mean, about — loving me? Asking me to be your fiancée for the purpose of getting married?

RON: Oh yes, Eth.

ETH: It was so *romantic* the way you said it.

RON: (*nods*) Been even better if we'd got two seats together.

ETH: Oh, Ron ... (*she lays her head on his chest*) I feel so at peace with my head snuggled against the haven of your pullover.

RON: Me too, Eth ... mind your ear on my holiday-camp badge.

ETH: I don't care. (*Contented sigh*) ... Mmmm ...

RON: Pardon?

ETH: Just — mmm ... Ron, there's an awful *draught* coming from somewhere.

RON: Perhaps there's a *hole* in my pullover.

ETH: No, it's a door open somewhere. (*Sits up*) Yes, look. The front door. Somebody's left it wide open. No wonder I'm frozen!

RON: (*considering the problem*) ... Tell you what, Eth.

ETH: What?

50

SHE LIKES AN ENGAGEMENT RING

BUT NOT A MARRIAGE ONE

Address your letters to Miss Madge Denison, "Red Star Weekly," 12 Fetter Lane, Fleet Street, London, E.C.4.

Make your letters brief, but give all the facts. Sign your letters with a pen-name, but your full name and address must be enclosed. All letters will be treated as confidential, and replies can only be given in the paper.

Dear Miss Denison,—I am twenty-four and have been engaged twice to the same girl. She broke it off the first time a month before our marriage, then wanted to make it up. I gave her back her ring.

Well she let me go on arranging about another home, and now I can see her, within a few weeks of marriage, cooling off again. I am bitterly disappointed and angry, as I do not wish to be made a fool of a second time.

I spoke to my girl's mother about it, and she confessed my girl had treated every boy she ever went with badly. I have treated my girl very well, and it is not that she is afraid of marriage. What shall I do? Shall I hope on that she will marry me, or stop all arrangements?—"JILTED ONCE ALREADY."

In your place I would make no further arrangements for the marriage. Just tell your girl you can see how the wind is blowing and save her the trouble of breaking it off with you by doing this yourself. It will bring her to her senses. It is difficult to say what her reason is for her changeableness. If she just wants the pleasure of courtship, but is jibbing at the responsibilities of marriage, you will be better off without her.

Bride-To-Be. — You should see your doctor. The discharge is not dangerous, but is better to be cleared up. At the same time mention the other matter to him. Don't be shy. He'll think nothing of it. And please accept my very best wishes for your future happiness.

John's Ex-Girl.—You are very young, and will probably meet someone else. I think you should try to put this boy out of your mind since there are objections to a friendship with him.

H. K. — For the sake of your two children, I think you should stay at home. It's not easy getting a situation where you could have the children with you and earn enough to bring them up decently.

Frightened Colleen.—Since the boy has so little control over his emotions, you must cut your goodnights very short and see to it that you are never alone for long. Take your pleasures in crowded places.

Raymond's Girl.—Yes, I think you are both a bit too young yet to be keeping company. Going around in a mixed crowd would be all right.

Worried.—What you used wouldn't help because it is intended to remove only greasy stains. Sponge the stained part with one part hydrogen peroxide to four parts warm water.

Brokenhearted. — Since you know in your own heart you do not run after the boy, never mind what people say. I wouldn't take him home, however, when your parents are out. Let your friendship develop naturally—don't try to rush it, especially as the boy is shy.

Unhappy Kate.—If it's a daily occurrence, I think you are quite right to be vexed, unless your husband has some purpose for it. Try to find out what he does. Could he be working somewhere? But on no account nag him. If you haven't enough to do, why not take a part-time job yourself? The money would come in useful, I am sure.

Irish Colleen.—Some of the boy's friends will give you his address, surely. Or contact his old employers. They may have been notified.

Brown Eyes, Bury.—Since the man is not free to accept your friendship, I think it is useless going on with it. You are only wasting your time and piling up unhappiness for yourself. Break away now and reshape your life without him. It will hurt, but time will heal the wound.

Fed-Up.—I really think the only solution is to strike out on your own and either go to live with friends or go into digs. I know this won't leave you much spare cash, but you'd be happier.

Worried Blue Eyes.—You should not try to cut your husband off from his friends. I'm sure the young man will find a girl soon, and then he'll have no time to spare for his men-pals.

Broken-Hearted.—You did wrong telling the boy you loved him. That is probably why he made such a suggestion to you. Of course you mustn't agree to it. Tell him quite frankly that unless he shows you more respect, you'll end the friendship. I think if you did decide to definitely put him out of your mind, you'd be much happier. Try to interest yourself in someone else. I don't really think the boy will change.

A FLY IN THE OINTMENT

Dear Miss Denison,—I have been going around with a young man for two months and have grown extremely fond of him. He's clever, upright and trustworthy—things on which I set great store. But there's a fly in the ointment. He is the type of person who doesn't give a hang about his appearance. At times he looks positively sloppy and this bothers me a great deal. I want to be proud of his appearance, but how can I when sometimes one could shovel the dirt out from under his nails? How can I approach him about this?—"SALLY 2."

Som... ... a good-humoured ... ticism will help ... ck. At the same ... re straightening ... off a jacket, or ... a loose hair ... he young man ... he could be if he ...

... f course, you ... the situation ... a chance on ... son's feelings. ... r in the long ... ct is over-... d qualities.

YELLOW POPPY.—By all means ask him to your party. I don't think you should make him your partner, though. You are bound to be the central figure and, being a complete stranger to the company, he might find it rather embarrassing to be in the limelight.

JANUARY JILL.—I'm afraid you're wasting your time. He seems to be very much in love with this other girl, and even if he wasn't, you have no reason to believe he would turn to you.

LAZYBONES.—Be a little more strong-minded in future. Make up your mind that nothing is going to make you miss that bus. Getting out of bed half an hour earlier might help, too!

WHITE LIE.—Tell your boy friend your real age next time you see him. I'm quite sure it won't affect his love for you.

TWO MEN HAVE SLIPPED THROUGH HER FINGERS ALREADY

A GIRL who gives Mary Lou as her pen-name writes to ask for some tips on how to hold her man. She's been disappointed twice already and doesn't want to lose this one, whom she loves dearly.

Well, Mary Lou, don't try to own your man. By that I mean don't be too possessive towards him. The average man doesn't like this. Many a girl who, after a date or two with a man, finds herself eager for the engagement ring to be placed on her finger and shows this eagerness too much, ends up with the young man beating a hasty retreat. Men seem to sense when a girl is about to put the "I own you" sign on them and shy away from it.

Be friendly and charming but be careful not to give your boy the impression that you are over-anxious.

If you get as far as becoming engaged, still give him sufficient leeway. You can naturally expect to have his exclusive attention as far as dates are concerned, since this is your right as his fiancee. But don't start bossing him around. If he gets a taste of this before the wedding bells, he may g... Disillusioned Girl ...

Disillusioned Girl.

I am sorry you have had these unhappy experiences with both boy friends, but you are quite right, my dear. Sex experience should never be allowed before marriage, no matter what a young man says. It is the girl who suffers every time, and even if no baby is created, the girl herself never feels the same again and often becomes very unhappy. Read "Why Are Sex Relations Wrong Before Marriage?" price 9d., which explains this. I feel sure that the right young man will come along who has the same code of behaviour as yourself.—Mary (Louth).

RON: I'll go and *close* the door.

ETH: Will you, sweetheart?

RON: (*getting up*) Just leave the whole thing to me. (*Leaves*)

ETH: (*to herself, fondly*) He's so practical. It just all seems too good to be true.

The front door bangs shut.

RON: (*returning; briskly*) Well, that's that little job jobbed.

ETH: Thank you, beloved. (*Coy*) Now come and claim your reward. Our first *engaged* kiss.

RON: Oh, Eth …

ETH: Mind noses!

A big kiss — in the middle of which comes an urgent banging on the front door.

RON: (*soft*) Eth — can you hear my heart pounding?

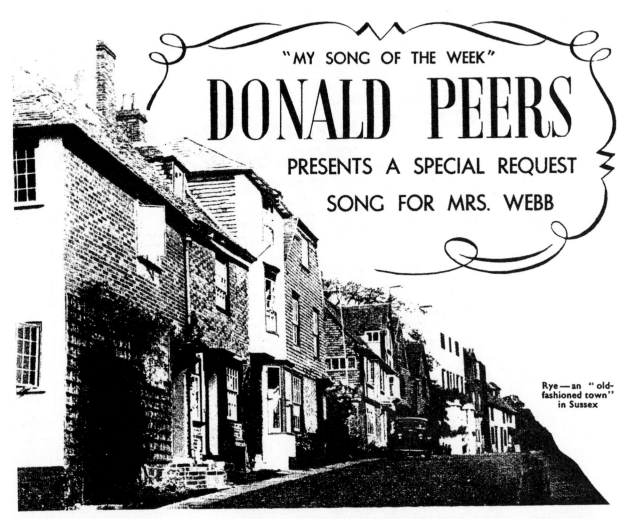

"MY SONG OF THE WEEK"

DONALD PEERS

PRESENTS A SPECIAL REQUEST

SONG FOR MRS. WEBB

Rye — an "old-fashioned town" in Sussex

IN AN OLD-FASHIONED TOWN

(They return to their kiss. The front door bell rings)

RON: (*puzzled*) I wonder what part's making *that* noise?

ETH: It's the front door. There's somebody ringing. Ron, hadn't you better answer it?

RON: All right. (*He gets up, leaves*)

The doorbell rings again.

RON: Coming! Coming!

Ron goes out to the hall, opens the front door. There's Mr Glum — furious.

MR GLUM: Ron!

RON: (*surprise*) Dad! ... Ooh, Dad, you won't half cop it coming home this time of night.

MR GLUM: (*livid*) Coming home? I bin out at the gate looking for *you*! Where you bin? Half out my *mind* with worry! Rang up the police, the hospital, the People's Dispensary for Sick Animals ... have you no consideration?

RON: It's all right, Dad, I —

MR GLUM: All right? Gone half past three in the morning? It is *not* all right. A member of the Glum household hanging round the streets till after the last trolley bus! May I remind you that our family enjoys a certain reputation round these parts. And I'm trying to live it *down*. (*He starts to undo his leather belt*)

RON: (*fearfully*) Dad, why are you —

MR GLUM: You'll find out! You need to be taught that while you are living within my roof, you're still under my jurisprudence. Come on — (*he drags him from the hall into the front room*) Now — I want a complete explanation of why you — (*catching sight of Eth, falters*) ... you ... you ...

ETH: (*nervously*) Good evening.

MR GLUM: ... Ha*llo*, hallo, ha — it-all-becomes-clear-now — LLO! Oh, Ron! Ron, I am not easily shocked. But to come in my own front room and find *this* sort of thing. A love-nest!

ETH: It is *not* a love-nest!

RON: It's her hat.

MR GLUM: That's enough out of you! And as for you, young woman, I demand an explanation of what you're doing here with my son at this hour.

ETH: Well, what happened was —

MR GLUM: (*shout*) I don't believe a word of it! Pack of rotten lies!

RON: Now, Dad, you mustn't talk to ...

MR GLUM: (*hiss*) Will you keep your voice down? (*Whisper*) Do you want the whole neighbourhood to know of your dissolute goings-on?

RON: (*whisper*) What dissolute goings-on?

MR GLUM: (*bellow*) Locking your father out so you can mess about with a palone!

ETH: He didn't lock you out, Mr Glum. We came here specially to talk to you. You see, Mr Glum, Ron and I, we've just become — Ron, I think it's *your* place to tell your father.

RON: Tell him what, Eth?

ETH: (*shy*) What — what happened in the cinema tonight.

RON: Oh ... (*awkwardly*) Well, Dad ... it just all happened very *suddenly*, Dad. Just a bit of talking, then — *zonk*!

MR GLUM: Zonk?

RON: (*excited*) A burning arrow! (*Voice rising*) It was Comanches! Thousands of 'em — riding through the gulch and —

ETH: No, Ron, I didn't mean the picture. Mr Glum — what your son was trying to say is — tonight, him and me, we — got *engaged*!

MR GLUM: (*takes it big*) Engaged!

RON: Yes, Dad. And I wanted *you* to be the third to know.

ETH: Third, dearest?

RON: Well, you and me knew first.

MR GLUM: (*tragic*) What a blind trusting fool I've been! I should have guessed! That *was* face-powder on his lapel! And there's me thinking he'd just been blowing down his sherbert-dab! Well — (*fiercely turning on Eth*) — you're not having him!

ETH: Mr Glum —

MR GLUM: If you think for one minute I'd allow my only son to engage himself to a female of *your* ilk!

ETH: What's wrong with my ilk?

MR GLUM: The ilk that brings a lad home this hour of the night. Engaged? I should cocoa!

ETH: But I *love* him, Mr Glum.

MR GLUM: That is quite irreverant! How can Ron *consider* getting engaged to be married? He can't even support *himself*. *Look* at him. Can you really envisage him ever being in a position to keep a wife and home? Gaw — if it wasn't so laughable, it'd be comic.

ETH: Well, I happen to believe he *will* be able. I've known Ron long enough now to have every confidence in him. After all, we've been walking out for six months, Mr Glum.

MR GLUM: Then you can just walk out *again*. Through that door.

RON: No, Dad.

MR GLUM: Go on — off out of it! And if I ever catch you hanging round this boy again — I warn you. I have intimate connections with the Vice Squad.

Jungle Bride

When their plane crashes in the South American Andes, Jill Devon and Rick Carter make their way to a hidden valley inhabited by the "lost tribe" of white Indians. Another Englishman, Renegade Tom, who has been living with the Indians, tries to steal jewels from the Sacred Temple, and the three of them are bound to the stake. But Bobo, Jill's pet monkey, frees them and they escape into the forest. There they meet an explorer, David Heath. Rick finds Tom still has some of the jewels and takes them from him, vowing to return them to the Temple. Suddenly they are surrounded by the Indians, who take them back to the valley. The jewels are found on Rick. He is condemned to die and Jill is to marry the chief's son on the same day. David Heath gives her a stick of dynamite, which she flings into the funeral fire. There is a terrific explosion and, in the confusion, Jill frees Rick. A crash is heard and the natives find Renegade Tom, again stealing jewels from the Sacred Snake in the Temple, has been crushed to death as the stone idol fell on him. It is decided that Jill must marry the chief's son to appease the idol.

The ceremony has hardly begun when a terrific storm breaks. Lightning splits the sky and torrents of rain descend as a howling wind rises

The natives are horrified to see the Sacred Temple struck by lightning and sliding over the cliff. Jill, Rick and David flee for their lives

Rick suggests they take shelter in the tunnel which led to the Temple. There he says "You're my bride, Jill. Remember that, if we never get out of here alive."

They come to the place where the Sacred Temple stood and stare in amazement at the destruction about them. The Sacred Snake lies at their feet.

Jill trips and falls. Rick tells David to run for his life, but stays with her. The Indians surround them just as the storm ends and a rainbow appears

Jill clings to Rick as they submit to their captors, and tells him of her undying love. This time they have no hope of ever seeing the outside of the valley again

Tall Trees begs his father to allow Jill to live. "She is my bride!" he cries. "Kill the man, but save my princess!" A great murmur goes up from the crowd

Slowly, the Sacred Snake is seen rising from the ground surrounded by flares of blazing light. "Behold!" the Chief cries "He wishes death to our prisoners!" (To be continued.)

ETH: Vice —? (*Blazing, advances on him*) Mr Glum, I am not used to being spoken to like that and I don't intend to. You might as well know now — bullying won't help you.

MR GLUM: (*a little taken aback*) Oh, I'm a bully now, am I? That's nice, isn't it? Being name-called by a chit of a girl within the privates of your own home. Well, I'm not bandying words with you any further. Ron, kindly inform this person her presence is no longer desirable here. (*Mr Glum turns away*)

RON: Right ho, Dad. Eth, Dad says your presents are no longer desirable here.

ETH: Then you just inform your father, Ron, you inform him that this is the 1950s, we're not living in Victorian times and if I want to see you I shall continue to see you, and no amount of threatening is going to make any *difference*.

RON: Right. (*Trying to remember it all*) Dad, Eth says this is the 1950s, we're not living in … (*thinks*)

MR GLUM: (*his back to him; prompting*) Victorian times.

RON: Victorian times. And — (*thinks*)

MR GLUM: And if she wants to see you, she will continue to see you.

RON: And if she wants to see me she will continue to see me. And — (*thinks*)

MR GLUM: And no amount of threatening is going to make any *difference*.

RON: And no amount of threatening is going to make any *difference*.

MR GLUM: (*turning to face Ron*) She ... said ... *what*? Never known such defiance! In that case, Ron, I forbid *you* to see *her*. Understand? Hereafter, you are never to see her again!.

ETH: (*appalled, urges Ron*) Ron ...?

RON: It's all right, Eth. Leave it to me. (*Bravely*) Dad, if you think you can keep Eth and me apart, you're wrong. (*Firmly*) There is no possible way you could stop me from seeing my Eth.

MR GLUM: No? Suppose I take your *trousers* away from you and hide them?

RON: (*reflective*) Oh yes, that's a good way.

ETH: Mr Glum, I — I had hoped this meeting would be very different. But if you choose to deny your son's happiness by removing his — nether *garment* ... well — on your own head be it! (*Biting back tears, she leaves*)

Music, and we go forward to the Glums' front room, ten days later, daytime.

Mr Glum is in chair, reading the Greyhound Express. As he turns over the page —

MR GLUM: (*calls*) Oh, Ron, do come away from there. You've had your face pressed against that window for the last ten days. Them net curtains will leave your nose permanently criss-crossed.

Ron enters from hall. He is without trousers.

RON: (*discontented*) ... I'm bored ... (*Elaborately casual*) Dad — could I have my trousers back just for a little while? I think I'll have a stroll down to the post office.

MR GLUM: What for?

RON: I fancy a tuppenny-halfpenny stamp.

MR GLUM: Ron, that's the eighteenth transparent excuse since breakfast! (*Mimicking*) 'Dad, I think I'll take the budgerigar for a walk'. 'Dad, I think I'll go to the lost property office and see if I've lost anything'. Do you think I don't know what you're trying to sneak out for? A candlestine meeting! Oh, Ron, — why don't you simply — forget her?

RON: Dad, I just — can't. Everything *reminds* me of her. Even when I was pumping my bicycle up this morning, the pump seemed to say 'Eth — Eth — Eth'. Dad, we love each other. She *told* me.

MR GLUM: Now, son, all I'm asking of you is — use a bit of common.

RON: They turned us off the common. That's why we went to the

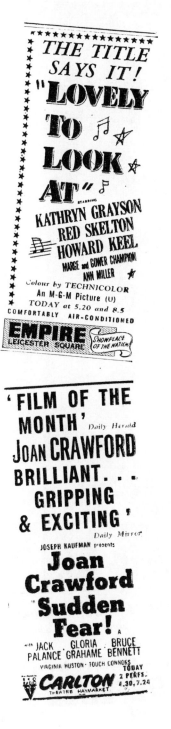
pictures. Dad, please don't ask me to forget her. It isn't possible. (*Passionate*) I'll never forget her. (*Dreamy*) For always engraved on my heart will be just the one name! (*Longish pause*)

MR GLUM: (*reminding him*) 'Eth'.

RON: Yes, that's the one.

Telephone rings.

MR GLUM: Answer that, Ron.

RON: (*lifts receiver*) Hallo.

A telephone box in the High Street, daytime.

Eth is inside.

ETH: Ron … ? Ron, listen carefully because I've got a lot to say. Is your father in the room with you?

RON: Yes.

ETH: Well, pretend this is a wrong number.

The Glums' front room.

RON: Right ho, Eth.

He puts the phone down.

MR GLUM: Who was it, Ron?

RON: Wrong number.

The telephone rings again. Ron lifts receiver.

RON: Hallo.

The telephone box.

ETH: Ron, I didn't mean 'put the phone down'. You'd better pretend it's somebody else calling. The butcher. Got that?

RON: Yes, Eth.

ETH: Not Eth. The butcher. Now listen. Ron, I've been to the Citizen's Advice and they say there's only one answer for us. What we've got to do —

Ron, phone to his ear, is listening intently.

RON: … Ooh! (*Glances at Mr Glum*) He won't like *that*. That'll make him ever so angry.

Mr Glum's face shows he's suspicious.

RON: (*into phone*) Well, if it's the only way — yes, I will. I'll do it.

MR GLUM: Who is it, Ron?

SPORT, Vol 15, No. 164

THE NATIONAL SPORTING MAGAZINE

MARCH 2nd—8th, 1951

SPORT

SHEFFIELD UNITED F.C., 1951

Back row: H. Hitchen,
Front row: G. Hutchinson,

24 PAGES

£20 TO B

WHI

WHICH BAI

RON:*Just a minute, Dad. (*Listens to phone*) 'Course I do. (*His voice softens*) I love you with all my heart. (*He puts the phone down*)

MR GLUM: Ron — who *was* it?

RON: The butcher, Dad.

MR GLUM: (*thoughtfully*) Oh, *was* it? Now was it really? How very interesting!

Music — and we return to the pub, night.

LANDLORD: But I take it it *wasn't* the butcher, Mr Glum. It was some *plan* she was getting up.

MR GLUM: Plan? I'll thank you not to dignify that diabolical machination she pulled as a 'plan'. Never have I been placed in a position of such degrading humiliation. A court of *law* — that's what I found myself in! Can you credit it? For the first time in our history, a member of the Glum family had his name dragged through a court of law!

LANDLORD: *First* time? What about that Uncle Charlie of yours?

MR GLUM: (*hotly*) Bigamy don't count! Uncle Charlie's not a criminal, he's just naturally affectionate. All nine of 'em want him back. To compare that with what they let me in for, just because I was trying to do what was best for my boy on account of his financial position.

LANDLORD: You haven't told me — how *was* he placed in that respect?

MR GLUM: Frankly, Ted, he was not placed at all. Financially, he couldn't even get to the starting-gate. But next thing I knew, through the post comes — well, with a bit of luck it should still be in my brief-case.

Mr Glum leans down and picks up a brown paper carrier bag. Rummaging through it —

MR GLUM: (*tut-tutting*) Oh, what a lot of useless things one accumulates, eh, Ted? Things you *know* you'll never use but you just can't bring your-self to discard. Look at *this.* (*Exhibits envelope*) Self-Denial Envelope ... Ah! (*Brings out document*) *This* is what Eth had engineered for me to get through the post. (*Shows it to landlord*)

LANDLORD: Strike me rotten! A summons!

MR GLUM: Exactly! And not, you'll notice, the normal non-payment-of-rates summons all self-respecting householders might expect this time of year. No — just *see* what this one said. (*Points out wording*) "Take notice that Ronald Crippen Glum has applied to this Court for consent to be married on the grounds that you being the person whose consent is required have refused consent. You are entitled to appear and oppose the application which will be heard on Friday before the Abbotsbury Road Magistrates.' See what he'd done, Ted? Wilfully — with malice and aforethought — taken me to court! His own *father!*

LANDLORD: Tt! How you must have felt!

MR GLUM: I can't tell you, Ted! The shame! The iggominy! 'Course I had to *go* — no choice. But I'll never forget that morning. Ron and Eth, they'd got to the court before me and there they were in one of them ante-rooms ...

Music — and we go to Magistrates' Court waiting-room, daytime.

Ron and Eth are sitting alone on a bench.

ETH: Oh Ron ... I hate the thought of doing this to your father as much as you do. But he's only got himself to blame. It's time he was taught you are now an adult.

RON: Exactly what I told him, Eth. I said quite firmly, I said, 'Look, Dad, you got to realize I am now a grown-up adult with all an adult's desires and capabilities'.

ETH: When did you tell him that?

RON: When he was peeling the silver paper off my Easter egg.

ETH: Well, if he's been told, then I've no sympathy. He brought the whole thing down on his own *head*, didn't he, beloved?

RON: No, Eth. He brought it down on my head.

ETH: Not the Easter egg, Ron. The summons. That's why we've simply *got* to win this case. So before we go *into* court, dearest, would it help you if we went through a few of the preliminaries?

RON: Oh yes, Eth.

ETH: No, Ron, I didn't mean that way —

RON: Go on, Eth, just a kiss ... just for friendly ...

ETH: No, Ron, not here, it's contempt of court, we could be —

Mr Glum enters scene.

MR GLUM: 'Allo, 'allo, 'allo! Well, what a touching picture. Like a scene from Hans Andersen. The two little ill-treated, 'ard-done-bys — 'Andful and Grapple.

ETH: Mr Glum, there's no call to take that attitude.

MR GLUM: You'll be surprised how much attitude I'm going to take. For your information, I intend to fight this case through every court in the land. See this briefcase? (*Holds up brown paper carrier bag*) Know what it's bulging with? Something that'll keep your precious Ron quiet for a very long time to come.

RON: Oh, Eth, he's brought my Easter egg!

MR GLUM: I wouldn't bring *you* nothing! These are my *legal* notes! I went out and bought that *Every Man His Own Lawyer* book and I've been up all night copying the lot *out*, the *lot*! I'll show Ron what it means to pit his wits against mine. Be like a contest between a pram and a furniture van.

ETH: But Mr Glum, Ron's *not* trying to make you look small. There's nothing personal in that summons.

MR GLUM: Nothing personal? My own *son*! When I think of all the *love* I

lavished on that boy. Not a bag of liquorice all-sorts I didn't save him my coconut ones. Never a bowl of stewed apples did he have, I didn't spend hours taking out all the toenail bits. And those days when there wasn't enough pilchards to go round, who was it went without just so you could *have* one?

RON: The cat, Dad.

MR GLUM: Well, who *fought* the cat to get them off its saucer? And this is how you repay that devotion. Oh, the Good Book had it right. 'How sharper than an ungrateful tooth is a serpent's child!'

Court attendant opens door from court-room.

ATTENDANT: All right, we're ready for the next case.

A VOICE FROM WITHIN COURT: Call Ronald Glum.

ATTENDANT: (*to Mr Glum*) Would you be Ronald Glum?

MR GLUM: Not for a king's ransom, mate. (*Indicating Ron*) This is your man, Inspector.

ATTENDANT: (*indicating door*) Through here, sir. (*As Ron and Eth leave*) You Mr Glum?

MR GLUM: Right.

ATTENDANT: Fag!

MR GLUM: Eh?

ATTENDANT: Fag!

MR GLUM: Sorry, I ain't got a spare one.

ATTENDANT: I mean put yours out. (*Nods him through door*)

A small informal court-room, daytime.

MAGISTRATE: (*to his clerk*) I'll take the matter of the Glum application for marriage consent next. Is either of the parents present?

MR GLUM: Yes, me lud. I am, me lud.

MAGISTRATE: Mr Glum, may I point out — I am not 'me lud'.

MR GLUM: Then you want to watch it, mate. You won't half catch it if he comes in finds you sitting in his chair.

MAGISTRATE: No, Mr Glum, I am a magistrate. You will therefore address me as 'your Worship'.

MR GLUM: Oh. I crave the court's indulgence. (*Brings out document with his speech on it; reads*) Your Worship, gentlemen of the jury, the evidence I shall put before you will be of such a nature as to demand the supreme —

MAGISTRATE: Mr Glum!

MR GLUM: *Now* what?

MAGISTRATE: Mr Glum, in the first place we have no jury, in the second place you will not speak until you're asked to speak. Now will you please sit down.

MR GLUM: But look here …

MAGISTRATE: SIT DOWN, Mr Glum!

MR GLUM: All right. (*To himself*) And they call this justice! We who gave our legal system to the world!

MAGISTRATE: I would like to hear from the applicant for consent.

ETH: Ron, that's you.

RON: What is, Eth?

ETH: The magistrate wants to *hear* from you.

RON: Oh. (*Calls*) Hallo, your Worship!

ETH: No, Ron, you must step into that sort of booth there.

Ron enters witness box.

ATTENDANT: Will you take this card, raise your right hand and read what it says.

RON: Right ho. (*Takes card in right hand, raises it, squints up at it*) It's a bit far away.

ATTENDANT: No, put the card in the other hand.

RON: The other hand. (*Transfers card, keeps right hand in air*)

ATTENDANT: Now read the words on the card.

RON: Right … (*pause*)

MAGISTRATE: (*looking up from notes*) Well?

RON: I've read them, your Worship. What do I do now?

MAGISTRATE: Read them out loud.

RON: Oh, out loud. (*Reads*) Printed by the Hoxton Press, London E1.

ATTENDANT: (*mutter*) The other side of the card. It's the other *side* of the ruddy card.

MAGISTRATE: I think, Mr Usher, as this is an informal domestic matter, we can dispense with the swearing.

RON: 'Ruddy' isn't swearing, your Worship. Swearing is, like —

MR GLUM: Your Worship! May I be permitted to ejaculate an interception at this juncture?

MAGISTRATE: What is it, Mr Glum?

MR GLUM: I would like the court's permission to call a qualified handwriting expert.

MAGISTRATE: What on earth for?

MR GLUM: I can't read me notes. I had some margarine sandwiches in the briefcase and the paper's gone all transparent.

THE FOOTBALL INDUSTRY

Football again! What does it matter that only our horses were well-fed enough to win gold medals at Helsinki? Heroes of our own are going to win the championship, and the Cup. Home-grown villains are going down to Division II. On Saturday the great annual winter drama starts to unfold

by DENZIL BATCHELOR

JUST when the weather gets really fit for cricket the whistle cheeps, the nets sprout goal posts, and every one of the million people who watch League football every Saturday is inflated with the conviction that before bedtime he will have made enough from pools to give up work for life.

The new season opens with a flourish of trumpets, in a blaze of excitement. Which, among the 92 League sides, will be the teams of the year? Who, among the 3,493 paid players, will be the individual stars—and which ~~~gers will make history? Where d~~~ ~~~rnationally? Are we the ~~~ the dazzling unorthodoxy ~~~wing old, bowed down ~~~at by the United States ~~~s amateurs) by Luxem-~~~here be new tactics on ~~~ame the entertainment ~~~rices are going up, and ~~~ Are the players, those ~~~ast green carpet who ~~~ some £6 million a ~~~rds and their condi-

~~~**OR MONEY!**

~~~We know about ~~~tle are a side who ~~~s being beaten in ~~~counted as a sur-~~~d by the fact that ~~~ Simpson and ~~~ve even on their ~~~all careers are ~~~ are Chelsea, ~~~uch of a fairy ~~~ sweating on ~~~ Also under ~~~ Wednesday, ~~~ Plymouth ~~~ Third

Sheffield Wednesday's Jack Sewell
The Blades are sharp, and reckon their £34,000 was well spent on the inside-right.

Sheffield Wednesday's Derek Dooley
The 21-year-old who shot 46 goals in League games, one in a Cup-tie. Raw but effective.

~T Can Still Raise a Smile Before the Kick-off
~manager. It's his task to lead the Club out of the wilderness.
~hat's wrong with the side at present. Who couldn't?

Chelsea's John McNichol
He comes from Brighton. His job is to make openings for Roy Bentley.

Swansea Town's Ivor Allchurch
The inside-left's shrewd ball control helped to stave off relegation from Division II.

MAGISTRATE: Mr Glum, you must not keep interrupting.

ETH: May *I* say something, your Worship?

MAGISTRATE: Who are you?

ETH: If it pleases your Worship, I am the fiancée.

MR GLUM: And what are you if it don't please him? (*Laughs*)

MAGISTRATE: Mr Glum, although this hearing is informal, it is not the four-ale bar.

MR GLUM: More's the pity.

MAGISTRATE: I beg your pardon?

MR GLUM: And so you should.

ETH: Your Worship, may I say that's how he *always* is. Browbeating like that. He just won't *listen*, your Worship. Ron and I told him over and over, there's no reason at all why we shouldn't get married.

MR GLUM: What do you mean, 'no reason at all'? What you think you're gonna live on? Don't imagine you're coming to stay with us, 'cos I'm not having *that*. There's not going to be three of us borrowing off Mrs Glum.

ETH: Nobody suggested coming to live with you —

MR GLUM: Where else can you afford to live? Your Worship, I honestly don't know what you're messing about all this time for — how can they possibly get married when they won't have two ha'pennies to rub together?

ETH: But we *will* have each other. Won't we, Ron?

RON: Yes, your Worship. We'll have each other to rub together. (*He still has his right arm up*)

MAGISTRATE: Just the same, young man — and unless you're indicating a need to leave the courtroom, you can put that hand down now — just the same, your father has made what appears to be a valid point. Do you understand what your being married entails?

RON: No, your Worship.

MAGISTRATE: No?

RON: I understood what I'm being married in a blue suit.

MAGISTRATE: I was referring to your earning potential. Is your present occupation reasonably secure?

RON: Oh yes, sir. I've been at it for five years now. With a bit of luck I should be able to stay at it till I retire.

MAGISTRATE: What are you then?

RON: I'm unemployed.

As Magistrate frowns —

ETH: But *I'm* in work, your Worship. Good work, with prospects.

MAGISTRATE: I see. But what are you going to start off married life on? Have either of you any kind of a nest-egg?

RON: I haven't even got an Easter egg.

ETH: Your Worship, may I say that, as it happens, I *have* got a nest-egg!

MR GLUM: (*startled*) You what!

ETH: In my Post Office Home Safe, your Worship. Over the last six months I've been secretly saving up and I've now got approximately fifty pounds eleven and tuppence. (*Opens bag, brings it out*) Here.

MR GLUM: What? Here, you never *told* me about that.

MAGISTRATE: It makes quite a difference, Mr Glum. With a sum like that to start them off — I see no reason at all why your son and this obviously very capable young woman should not become man and wife.

MR GLUM: (*angry*) You see no reason why not? They went and *summonsed* me, that's why not!

MAGISTRATE: Mr Glum, I'm getting a little tired of these outbursts. You seem to look on this whole matter merely insofar as it affects your own self-esteem. My concern is for these two young people — and their happiness.

MR GLUM: (*bewilderment*) What on earth's *happiness* got to do with it? We're talking about *marriage*.

MAGISTRATE: Mr Glum, because I'm just about reaching the end of my tether with you, I am going to grant the court's consent to this marriage. (*Clears throat*) Ronald Crippen Glum, by the powers vested in me under the Guardianship of Infants Act 1925, I have pleasure in granting consent to your marriage. (*He signs a form — it's handed to Ron by clerk. During which —*)

RON: Oh, Eth ...

ETH: Ron — we've done it! We've got the money and we've got the consent. (*Inspects form*) Nothing can stop us now!

MR GLUM: I protest! Your Worship, I most fervidly protest. I shall lodge an objection with the stewards.

ETH: Oh, Mr Glum, don't be a bad loser. Can't we make friends now?

MR GLUM: Make friends! It's the biggest carve-up since the Dreyfus case! (*Shout*) J'accuse!

ETH: Don't, Mr Glum! You keep on like that, he'll be having you for contempt of court.

MR GLUM: Contempt of — ? Wait a minute, what did they say about that in my Home Lawyer book? (*Scrabbles among his papers*)

ETH: Your Worship, may I say one more thing?

MAGISTRATE: Certainly.

ETH: My husband and I — my *future* husband and I — we will try to prove worthy of the trust you have placed in us.

MAGISTRATE: I'm sure you will. (*To clerk*) If the next case is ready —

MR GLUM: Just hang on a minute, if you don't mind, your Worship, may I say one more thing, too?

MAGISTRATE: Yes, Mr Glum?

MR GLUM: You call yourself a magistrate? You couldn't try a pair of boots on!

MAGISTRATE: (*incredulous*) What's that? What did you say?

MR GLUM: Hard of hearing too, eh? They should have turned you out to grass years ago!

MAGISTRATE: Have a care, Mr Glum!

MR GLUM: (*mimicking*) 'Have a care, Mr Glum!' Bald-headed old barrister!

MAGISTRATE: Mr Glum — one more word and I shall hold you in contempt.

MR GLUM: Not half the contempt I hold you in! Great four-eyed capitalist git! Servile lackey of the boss classes!

MAGISTRATE: That does it! Mr Glum, it may surprise you to hear of the maximum sentence I'm able to impose for this offence.

MR GLUM: Oh, no it won't, mate. (*Waves notes*) Got it here in black-and-white. (*Reading*) 'Maximum sentence for contempt of court is £50'.

ETH: Fif —? Oh, Ron!

MR GLUM: (*reading*) 'Failure to pay which means committal to prison till such time as the contempt is purged'. And where's a poor man like me going to find that kind of money of a Thursday?

RON: Oh, Eth — no! Don't let them send my Daddy to prison!

MR GLUM: (*stretching out his wrists*) So on with your shackles, jailer. Consign me to your dungeon.

RON: (*lifting money, pleading*) Eth —?

ETH: (*nodding tearfully as she slowly tears up Consent Form*) Oh, Ron ...!

As Mr Glum smiles in satisfaction, playout music, and BLACKOUT.

CORONATION CLOSE-UP . . .

The Duchess of Kent and her daughter, Princess Alexandra, drive to the Abbey in the procession of Princes and Princesses of the Blood Royal.

Holding the Orb, the smiling Queen leaves the Abbey yesterday in the State Coach.

Here's a health unto her Majesty

Royal footmen, dressed in glittering uniforms instead of their usual blue battledress, raise their glasses in a toast to the Queen.

"Here's a health unto her Majesty. . . ."

It went round the world last night.

From gay, golden, crowded

THE MULTITUDE SANG, THE TRUMPETS SOUNDED— THE QUEEN WAS CROWNED

PRINCE CHARLES SEES CROWNING

(There was even a burst of sunshine while they were in the Abbey)

By NOEL WHITCOMB

THE VOICE OF BRITAIN RANG OUT ONCE MORE PROUDLY THROUGH THE WORLD, RAISED IN TRIUMPHANT SONG, AS QUEEN ELIZABETH WAS CROWNED IN WESTMINSTER ABBEY YESTERDAY.

And a new sun shone in this reawakened land—the burning one of fifty million faces—shaming the sun, which was hiding.

Drenched in a while The little boy's eyes grew

PAGE 2 DAILY MIRROR, Wednesday, June 3, 1953

THE DUKE WAITED AT THE DOOR . . .

His look, his touch said: Well done!

By AUDREY WHITING

IT was a kind of extraordinary depth and infinite understanding.

It was a glance that lasted for three seconds and brought tears of homage to the eyes of the newly-crowned Queen Elizabeth with a speech without words by the Duke of Edinburgh that said the whole world was watching at once, her husband was as very proud of his wife.

The great Coronation service over, the Duke waited quietly before the crown entrance door of the two adjoining Royal retiring chambers in the Abbey Annexe for the arrival of the Queen.

Before the door closed the Queen walked and lightly held his white arm and her elbow as they walked.

And the Queen smiled gently.

Then, as bells were heard ringing from churches all over the land, nearly people had five out and crowded round together. The only five moments of a breathing space in the whole day.

They first stepped to the newly-come together to the Silver in the forth service. With the Duke of Edinburgh she said this.

Once he touched the diamond necklace and pendant around her throat and said to lower and gave her majesty's head.

The family raised champagne glasses, and drank a toast loud to her Majesty.

After lunch came the portraits, five minutes, the Queen, with the Duke, smiled beside the table and went into her own accord.

For a few minutes, as of time when she wanted done, for personal need. the Queen and the Duke talked quietly together.

LITTLE STREETS TO SEE HER

THE Queen and the Duke of Edinburgh, will drive today through Northern and London—five of four great Coronation drives through the capital.

THE ELOPEMENT

Summer For Growing Up

by SHEILA FRAZER
ILLUSTRATION BY WALTER SROR

Peta would remember this holiday as a milestone in her life. For the first time, a door to the future had been opened through which she had taken her first faltering step

IN the little attic bedroom high up under the eaves, Peta stood before the rosewood - framed mirror—a pair of scissors in one hand, a plait of glossy, blue-black hair in the other.

The cutting-off of the hair was to have made her look older; but instead her face—framed by the dark, straight, short hair—looked narrower and more childish than ever. Even in the dimly lighted room the freckles marching across her nose

She saw that his eyes were charged with an emotion that she could not fully understand. In that same instant she stepped over the boundary from adolescence into womanhood

"Would it be acceptable," he said gravely, "if I asked you for a kiss?" She opened her arms wide and flung them round him

13

ift

en cursed
h beauty
tal,
brilliant,
was
wrecking
her whole life

The pub, night. Pub hubbub ... while landlord is calling 'time' he has one resentful eye on Mr Glum who is whispering lasciviously into the ear of a giggling barmaid, Rosie.

LANDLORD: (*shouting*) Time, gentlemen, please. All your glasses. Drink up now, gents ... Mr Glum — *please*! (*Pointedly*) Shouldn't you be getting home to your lawful-wedded *wife*?

MR GLUM: (*from barmaid's ear, blissfully*) Oh, Ted, have a heart. Would you ask a man to go from Dreamboat to Tugboat?

LANDLORD: All very well, but I need my barmaid for these glasses. (*Rosie, with a last giggling moue at Mr Glum moves away*) Don't understand you, Mr Glum. All evening you been sitting there wiping your moustache on Rosie's neck. What you two been doing all that whispering about?

MR GLUM: (*fondly*) Memories, Ted. Just — memories.

LANDLORD: (*crossly*) Giggling to yourselves the whole night — proper *spectacle* it was.

MR GLUM: But a very *pleasant* spectacle where Rosie's concerned. When she laughs, so much of her has a good time.

LANDLORD: Should have thought you'd have more important matters occupying your mind. What with your son's wedding looming up so near.

MR GLUM: Don't remind me of that, Ted, please don't remind me. The only cheerful thing that can be said for them nuptial arrangements is they're driving me to drink. So put another brown in there.

LANDLORD: They've been getting you down, then?

MR GLUM: Well, Eth has. Her nerves have been under more strain than Rosie's satin skirt. In fact, it got so bad that last Thursday — no, if you'll place an additional brown on standby, I'll go back further. Last *Tuesday*. There was Eth, in our front parlour — and she had a face as long as a gasman's mac ...

Music — and we hark back to the Glums' sitting-room, evening.

Ron and Eth are on the sofa.

ETH: Oh, Ron — this *latest* carry-on about who's going to be bridesmaids! Now Aunt *Hetty's* offended because I'm not having Maureen.

RON: Oh. How much reen are you having?

ETH: Maureen's her little daughter ... 'Little'? Ha-*ha*!

RON: Ha-ha! (*Laughs*) What we laughing at, Eth?

ETH: That Maureen is fourteen stone, Ron. What do I want fourteen stone clumping down the aisle behind me for? But I'm only the bride. I've got *no* say. Whose *day* is it? That's what I'd like to know. Whose day *is* it?

SHORT STORY by BARBAR

I love him

I love him

I love him not

She was in love with life now, more than ever. Before she met Henry she had been in love with life but never in love with a man

RON: ... St. Swithin's?

ETH: Not *today*, pet. I mean the wedding-day. Honest, it's as though that doesn't concern *us* any more. It's just other people.

RON: Oh, Eth, don't keep thinking about it.

ETH: What else *can* I think about?

RON: Well, let's see if I can think of something for you to think about. (*Pause*) ... Cowboys?

ETH: Oh, Ron, I wish I could have your gift for adapting yourself to circumstances. But, dearest heart, I've got into such a state of nerves. (*Sob*) I just don't care any more, I just don't ... (*cries*)

RON: Oh, don't cry, Eth. Please don't cry. You'll make my fountain-pen clip go rusty.

Door opens, in comes Mr Glum.

MR GLUM: 'Allo, 'allo, 'allo! Oh, lummy, not again! Whenever I come in, you two are either having a good cry or a good try. Well, cheer up, Eth. (*Brandishing sheet of paper*) I've been working on the list of wedding-guests. You'll be glad to know I've managed to widdle it down to a reasonable forty-two.

ETH: Well, that's one blessing. My mother couldn't get it lower than two hundred and twelve.

MR GLUM: I told you she should have left it to me. I got it down to manageable proportions in no time. (*Exhibiting list*) I just knocked *them* off for a start. Then *them*. And them. *And* them. And we can dispense with *them*! And cross them out. And them! Give *this* couple the chop. Then them, them and them. And, finally — *them*. See? Easy.

ETH: But, Mr Glum — that's my whole *family*!

MR GLUM: Oh ... Then we *are* a bit snookered. 'Cos I'm not having none of *my* family struck off.

ETH: (*shrill*) And my family won't have any of *their* family struck off. And so it goes on and on. I'm just fed up with it! Why couldn't Ron and me just have a *quiet* wedding — just you and Mrs Glum and my parents and a few close friends?

RON: And me, Eth.

ETH: Oh, of course you, beloved.

MR GLUM: (*heat*) 'Cos you can't, that's why not. Talk about ingratitude. Here's your parents put themselves to the expense of las.ıing out for a high class society wedding —

ETH: A *what*?

MR GLUM: Go on — now tell me the Co-op *isn't* a society. They're having a hall and Bert Tozer's West End Rhythm Four and a cloakroom lady who doubles on vocals —

ETH: But I don't *want* all that ostentation and show! Oh, what Ron and me should do now if we had any sense is just *elope*, that's what we should do.

Greyhound Express

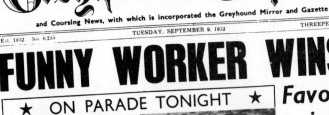

and Coursing News, with which is incorporated the Greyhound Mirror and Gazette

Est. 1932. No. 6,255   TUESDAY, SEPTEMBER 9, 1952   THREEPENCE DAILY

FUNNY WORKER WINS LEGER

Grand Prix Trial is divided

RACEGOERS CONSIDERED

ALTHOUGH the 2nd September Stayers' Stakes, which was to have taken place at Walthamstow to-night, failed to fill, visitors to the East London track will not go without the open races that are usually contested during the Tuesday meetings for the 2nd Grand Prix Trial Stakes will be run in two divisions.

The first division, due to be run at 9.18 p.m., is confined solely to locally-trained runners. This has brought together some of the best trackers in the country, among them Mrs C. H. Chandler's Kind Comrade, who is fresh back from his recent triumphs at Clapton, where he has won two impressive London trophy races over the 550yds course.

Won last week

When seen at Clapton last Thursday, Kind Comrade gave his supporters some qualms when running into trouble at the second bend, but this stout-hearted performer put in such a terrific finish that he won the race by three lengths, justifying the applause that was accorded him.

One from whom Kind Comrade will have most to fear is Green Wings, winner of last week's 1st Grand Prix Trial Stakes, who on Saturday evening clocked 30.14secs.

This speedy daughter of Trevs Cutter has been running at the top of her form lately, but, although she has been staying on in recent attempts, she may not be capable of holding off Kind Comrade.

Impressed

Division II has attracted Trainer Boswell's Lucky Blackbird, who created a very favourable impression when running in the heats of the Derby in June.

On that occasion he ran the speedy Ryton Basher to a short head after being in trouble. Since June, however, this son of Lucky Tanist has had little racing.

Beaten in the heats of the Chelsea Cup at Stamford Bridge on August 30, Lucky Blackbird was entered in an open race at Wembley last night. This outing should have benefited him to a great extent and, provided he gets a clear run, he has a great chance of winning tonight.

★ ON PARADE TONIGHT ★

TRIAL RUNNERS

Polar Star (left) and Lucky Blackbird who appear in the 2nd Grand Prix Trial Stakes, which is due to be run in two divisions at Walthamstow tonight.

Soccer star's dog may outrun rivals in kennel sweep

HIGHLIGHT of this evening's all-graded programme at Romford will be the kennel sweepstakes due to be run over 650yds. Apart from Candy and Flying Disc, who have been given more to do, the other four runners have been well matched by the grader.

The event should go to 'Spurs and English international full-back Alf Ramsey's greyhound Burning Desert, but in such an even field the verdict might well be in the balance until the last yard.

Burning Desert, who has won several races over this course, will probably set the early pace.

He stays on well and is expected to prove just good enough to hold off strong challengers in Dutton Sabre, Taurus Rowley and slow-starting but strong-running John Paul.

WAS UNLUCKY

Dutton Sabre, who is owned by Mr H. J. Bell and trained by Mrs Pett, has shown great improvement during the last few weeks and has beaten good fields over the shorter 460yds course.

He was unlucky to be beaten on the line over this course recently by Taurus Rowley after making most of the running. If he should obtain the lead during tonight's race he might well prove good enough to win.

Main sprint event is also expected to prove an exciting race for, apart from Chigwell Blue, who has been heavily penalised for her fast win on Saturday, the race appears very open.

Should the going be soft, it would favour Barmitzvah, who could lead throughout over a wide course.

However, he would have to be at his best, for Warden, a recent newcomer from New Cross, who has been purchased by Mr H. C. Ablitt, is also a smart trapper and could run on strongly near the rails to threaten Barmitzvah towards the finish.

A point of interest in the meeting is that two greyhounds, Eastlands Ruler and Spring Bruce, reared under the Romford management gift scheme, will be taking part in the third and fifth races respectively.

IRISH HOOLIGAN

IRISH HOOLIGAN, who dislocated a hock when pulling up at the sough after his race at Clapton on Thursday evening, has been sent to D. Gabriel, the veterinary surgeon at Ashford, Middlesex.

After an X-ray examination he stated that he was confident that it would mend.

It was Mr Gabriel who looked after Funny Manner when he broke a hock last December. Funny Manner still races in top-class company at Walthamstow.

CLUB CONSIDER CLAPTON RACE

The Stewards of the National Greyhound Racing Club are this week to consider the report of the Clapton stewards on the eighth race at that track last Thursday.

ALL OVER THE SAME DISTANCE

WITH no open race on the card, racing manager Leslie Cox has arranged a well-graded programme at Dagenham this afternoon. Each of the eight races will be run over the 460yds standard course, and in the first will be seen a former top-class Harringay stayer in Chickerell Bird.

This fawn daughter of Black Hat and Chickerell Baby is getting on in years, for she was whelped in September, '46, and the curtain-raiser should be won by Derryhawn Debonair, who could lead this opposition throughout.

Carefree Cliff, who arrived in Trainer Ernie Welch's kennels recently, is fancied to take the second race, for this greyhound beat a better-class field over 460yds at Romford on Saturday, outrunning both Driving Drama and Blue Robin from the third bend.

He is a smart trapper and should enjoy a clear course near the rails and run on well enough to score.

In the main event of the afternoon, Stockman, who took part in the open race over the same distance at Romford on Saturday, is expected to start favourite, and if trapping on his best, fast style would prove an extremely difficult proposition.

However, he may find one too good for him in Drumcummer Prince, who runs on well near the rails after a smart start.

Drumcummer Prince, who is owned by Mr P W Aherne, formerly raced at Clapton but is now under the care of Mrs Pett, who also trains the little bitch Rio Capricorna, another competitor this afternoon.

The latter is a strong runner who gives her best displays over this course.

Only four locals—and three race together

ONLY four local dogs are included among the eighteen competitors for New Cross's annual 600yds race, the Millwall Cup and three of them, Helenslea Pride, Working Alone and Gracies Bob have been drawn together in the first of the three heats due to be decided on Thursday.

First two in each heat will qualify for the final, the final, which, decided on Saturday, carries with it prize-money to the value of £150 and trophy for the winner.

HEAT I
1 Wayward Moose (Sherry, Rams.)
2 Helenslea Pride (Tidbury, New X)
3 Overlush Harvest (Howe, Private)
4 Gracies Bob (Tidbury, New Cross)
5 Working Alone (Pickering, New X)
6 Mad Martha (Holland, Private)

HEAT II
1 Mellow Mystery (Reves, White C)
2 Sainted Stranger (Merchant, Pr.)
3 Kiki Sue ....(Orton, Clapton)
4 Priceless Flo ......(Morris, Private)
5 Mad Trust ......(Parry, New X)
6 Ranjics Humoresque (O'Mea, P R.)

HEAT III
1 Raging Current (Orton, Private)
2 Coolafin ....(Orton, Wimbledon)
3 Ice Man ....(Spoot, New Cross)
4 Glittering Too ....(Knott, Private)
5 Bawnmore Branch (Mann, S B.)
6 Monachdy Darling F (Parry, W C)
Res Athos ......(Appleby, New Cross)
Champion Cosy (Appleby, N X)
Ball Car ......(Pickering, New X)

Favourite checks into trouble

MR GEORGE FLINTHAM gained his second St Leger victory when Funny Worker led throughout to win the 20th Wembley classic last night. Mr Flintham, who had been successful in 1937 with Grosvenor Bob, received a tremendous reception from the 30,000 people who witnessed the event.

A 6 to 1 chance, Funny Worker was never in danger after the second bend and, although not staying on very well, finished with three lengths to spare.

His time of 40.50secs. was slow, but the early speed he showed will gain him many admirers in the Select Stakes on Monday.

Despite being unfavourably drawn in trap three odds of 11 to 8 were laid on Magourna Reject and when the traps were released it appeared likely that he would justify them.

Second away, he showed good speed to the turn but checked up badly and Mad Miller ran into him. The pair lost several lengths at the 238yds mark.

Magourna again lost ground at the third bend and at halfway was still last, fifteen lengths behind Funny Worker, who at this time was four lengths in front of Shaggy Swank, with Malanna Mace five lengths further away, third.

Mad Miller had improved and was lying fourth, two lengths behind Malanna Mace. When on leaving steps the two came straight, Malanna Mace passed the Magourna dog, who had lost so much ground to make up and failed by some yards.

Both Mad Miller and Magourna Reject were running on strongly in the last furlongs, indeed but for Mad Miller being baulked 50yds from home, Mr W E Hughes' dog may well have been second. As it was he was beaten a head for fourth place by the fast-finishing Magourna.

WINNERS

"Valentine" gave his 200th winning selection at Wembley last night. Other winners given at the meeting were Lancer o' Leer, Drumman Rambler, Smart Prince, Town Trip and Mr Eric.

Southend expert, "Priory Park," gave Flighty Olive, Crowned Champion (double), Minorcas Hope (nap) and Flitter Light.

MR GLUM: Elope! I should cocoa! What? After all the invitations been printed and I've put the announcement in the *Greyhound Express*? Oh, no! Eth, you should be looking *forward* to the reception and the celebration. For one thing, it'll be the first opportunity your family and our family will have to get together and really *talk*.

RON: Dad, our family don't even talk to each *other*.

MR GLUM: They will, Ron. With a common enemy there.

ETH: But who wants all that money to be spent? My father frittering his savings away on bridesmaids' dresses and expensive catering and a red toastmaster, and you — you paying out for posh hire-cars and —

MR GLUM: Eth, my child, it's a parent's *privilege* to spend his money on ... (*pause*) ... *Who* pays out for the hire-cars?

ETH: Well, you, Mr Glum. It's always groom's father attends to cars.

MR GLUM: Is it? ... Eth, perhaps I was a little hasty about this question of eloping —

ETH: Oh, Mr Glum, with your help we could *do* it. I'm sure we could. If you could just get a car and drive us up to Gretna Green —

MR GLUM: Hang on, Eth. The only *point* of helping you is to *avoid* hiring cars. Now, let me put my thinking-cap on ...

Music — and we return to the pub, night.

It's now empty, save for the landlord and Mr Glum.

LANDLORD: You mean, Mr Glum, you actually assisted them two to elope?

MR GLUM: Don't anticipate me, Ted. First thing was to devise a *plan* for the elopement. A plan which would be absolutely Ron-proof. That's the same as fool-proof, only double-strength. Well, having devised it, I decided to put it into operation last night. So at nineteen hundred hours all troops assembled in my front parlour for a final briefing ...

Music — and we're back in the Glums' sitting-room, night.

ETH: All right, Ron, let's just rehearse what's going to happen later tonight.

RON: Right ho, Eth.

ETH: Oh, no, Ron — not now.

RON: Oh, go on, Eth — one of my butterfly specials.

ETH: No, Ron, not when I've just put on a mouth —

Mr Glum enters.

MR GLUM: All right, that'll do, you two. You're still under starter's orders! Now, look, I hit lucky this afternoon. If Ron's going to drive you all the way up to Gretna Green on my motor bike, you'll want the route.

So, here — a road-map! (*Tosses it to Eth*) Don't say General Glum doesn't think of everything.

ETH: But Mr Glum, this is a road-map of Devon.

MR GLUM: Is it? Oh, blast! I had to take it with me hands behind me 'cos the man was looking. Never mind, take it along anyway. Then if you happen to pass through anywhere mentioned on it, you'll *know* you're on the wrong road. Right, then, Eth — let's hear you repeat back your instructions.

ETH: Right. I go to bed at ten as normal — but I lie awake and wait till my mother's snoring settles to a steady note. Then I dress silently, put all my necessaries in a suitcase and wait quietly for the pebble Ron's going to throw up at my window.

MR GLUM: Good, very good. All right so far, Ron?

RON: Yes, thank you.

MR GLUM: Right. Now what happens at a quarter to two?

RON: ... 'Listen With Mother'?

ETH: Quarter to two in the *morning*, Ron! In the morning *tonight*!

RON: (*thoughtfully*) Oh. In the morning tonight.

MR GLUM: At a quarter to two precisely, Ron, you and me arrive, with the pebble and a ladder. (*Going to mantelpiece*) Pebble here. Ladder's outside. It's the one Uncle Charlie hired to do the laundry.

ETH: To do the laundry?

MR GLUM: He's also hoping to do the baker's and the chemist's the same night. We lean the ladder against your window, Ron throws the pebble up, down you come, jump on the motor bike I'll have waiting at the kerb, and then — hey for Gretna Green!

ETH: (*glowing*) It'll be a long, jolty ride — but we won't even *notice*, will we, Ron?

RON: Not if we sit on the hay. I'm getting a bit excited now, Eth.

ETH: You must stay calm, beloved, because we'll be working to split-second timing. Remember, Ron — a quarter to two exactly!

Music, and we go to a suburban street, night.

The street is empty. The church clock is chiming 4 am. Chimes carry over as we see Mr Glum hurrying along it, shining a torch on the gate-post numbers.

MR GLUM: (*calling back over his shoulder*) Do get a move on, Ron — we're an hour and three-quarters late already! ... (*He looks back, sees a laden Ron leaning against a lamp-post.*) Gawd, no — he's gone to sleep again! (*He hurries back to him*) Poor lad — he's never been up this late before. (*Shakes snoring Ron*) Hey — Lili Marlene! Get a move on! It's gorn four! (*They stumble on down the street.*) Thanks to you, Eth's been waiting hours! If you hadn't leaned the ladder against that trolley-bus, we wouldn't have had to run all the way to the depot to get it back. Now come on, walk faster.

RON: I can't walk faster, Dad. I'm carrying too much.

MR GLUM: Whose fault is that? You would insist on bringing your bagatelle! Won't be told, will you? What you need with a bagatelle-board on your honeymoon I can't — oh, I don't know though. And I'd be happier if I knew where your mother's got to. You'll be stuck if *she* don't turn up.

RON: Why?

MR GLUM: She's carrying the motor bike. I dursn't *ride* it 'cos of the noise. (*Scanning the gates*) Wish they marked these numbers more clearly, I can't — wait a minute, we're here. She is number twenty-three, isn't she?

RON: Yes, Dad. Twenty-three Albatross Avenue.

MR GLUM: At last! (*He opens gate. They tiptoe up the path.*) Very quiet now, Ron. Can you see Eth up at the window? (*They halt*) Ron, can you see her?

RON: (*eyes closed, is swaying*)

MR GLUM: (*shout*) RON! (*Whisper*) Ron! Wake up, you dozey ha'p'orth. Oh, give me that. (*He leans the ladder against the wall*) Easy does it. Now, Ron — the pebble.

RON: The pebble.

MR GLUM: Yes, come on. The pebble.

RON: The pebble.

MR GLUM: DON'T JUST — don't just stand there intoning 'The pebble'. *Throw* it.

RON: Dad, I haven't got it. I left it on the mantelpiece.

MR GLUM: That's clever. Now what we going to do?

RON: Let's go back to bed.

MR GLUM: (*bitter*) Oh, you're a right example of Eager Bridegroom, you are. Talk about young Lockinbar has come out in his vest. You'll just have to climb up the ladder and *tap* on her window.

RON: All right, Dad. (*Ron climbs up, disappears out of Mr Glum's sight.*)

MR GLUM: (*scanning roadway*) And do it quietly! Cor! I can't believe this time tomorrow I'll be shot of him. (*Calling up*) Ron — you up there yet? (*Shines torch upwards*) Oh, no!

What he sees is Ron, face against the ladder, fast asleep.

MR GLUM: Never known anyone with such a flair for oblivion. Come *back* here! (*He tilts ladder, tumbling Ron to the ground*) Get out of it, I'll go up meself. (*He replaces ladder, climbs up it.*)

MR GLUM: (*As Ron picks himself up — from above him*) Here we are, Eth. Eth! ETH ... ? Ron.

RON: Yes, Dad?

MR GLUM: (*from above*) I can't see her. I'll climb inside and have a scout round.

RON: Right ho, Dad. (*Pause . . . Ron looks round uneasily. To keep his spirits up, sings softly to himself*) 'Mr Dream Man — send me some sand' (*Pause*) . . . Dad! (*Pause*) Dad! Dad, come down now, it's dark.

ETH'S VOICE: Pss! Ron! Ron!

RON: Dad, something's saying 'Ron, Ron'!

ETH: (*entering*) Ron, it's me.

RON: Hallo, Eth!

ETH: Oh, Ron — I waited and waited so long, I came out and walked round the streets looking for you.

RON: Think I should let Dad know, Eth?

ETH: Is he up *there*?

RON: Yes, Eth. He's gone inside.

ETH: Then you'd better tell him very *quickly*.

RON: Why?

ETH: This isn't my house!

RON: But it said number twenty-three.

ETH: Albatross *Crescent*. I'm Twenty-three Albatross *Avenue*. This is where that awful barmaid at Mr Ted's pub lives.

RON: Oh, Eth . . . (*Calls*) Dad!

ETH: Come down quickly, Mr Glum!

MR GLUM: (*off*) Not likely!

RON: What do you mean?

He looks upward — to see Mr Glum in window, beside a negligéed Rosie.

MR GLUM: Take the ladder away, Ron, I'm all right!

As he blissfully pulls down the blind, playout music and BLACKOUT.

Artist's Model

CLOCK GOLF

Take a lesson from one of France's top models. First rule: Keep your eye on the ball.

The pub, night. Pub hubbub, over which:

LANDLORD: (*shouting*) Time, gentlemen, please. All your glasses, please. Finish up that brown now, Mr Glum. Here, Mr Glum, didn't I hear some kind of bad news about your son Ron last week? He's not been ill, has he?

MR GLUM: Oh, he's never *ill*, Ted. One thing you can say about that boy of mine is that nothing ever goes wrong with him *physically*. How can there, when there's no moving parts? No, what he inflicted on me was something much worse. What he — no, I really don't want to talk about it.

LANDLORD: Sometimes talking helps, Mr Glum. You know what they say? 'Two heads are better than one'.

MR GLUM: Well, if that's what they say — (*pushing two glasses at him*) — put one head on *this* and another head on *that*. If you really do want to know, Ted — well the commencement of it, as you might say, in a manner of speaking — that began last Monday when him and his fiancée was alone together in our front room — with Eth, as usual, conducting the chat-show …

Music, and we hark back to the Glums' sitting-room, night.

Ron and Eth are on the sofa.

ETH: Oh, Ron … you've been miles away from me all evening. You haven't even noticed what I've done to myself, have you?

RON: No, Eth.

ETH: Well, look. (*Gets off sofa, walks up and down*) When I walk, notice anything about my *legs*?

RON: They keep going past each other?

ETH: About what you can *see*. (*Shyly*) Ron — I've shortened my skirt! It — it doesn't make me look too sensuous, does it?

RON: No, Eth.

ETH: I didn't want to overdo it, Ron. One thing I hate, is to make myself cheap. Know what I mean?

RON: Oh yes, Eth. I did it this morning.

ETH: Made yourself cheap?

RON: I was chatting to the budgie.

ETH: I meant 'common' cheap, like — oh, Ron, you're still only half-listening to me. I can tell by your face. Beloved, I believe you're in the throes of some deep emotional turmoil. Are you?

RON: Yes, Eth.

ETH: Oh, Ron — what's happened?

RON: Eth, I — I've resigned from the Labour Exchange.

ETH: Ron! After all this *time*! How long has it been?

RON: Seven years, Eth. Seven whole years I've been going there every Friday to draw my unemployment pay. Always on time. All weathers. Never a word of complaint. Then, last Friday, just because I got thrown out of that job they sent me for —

ETH: That nice post as yo-yo demonstrator? Ron, you didn't tell me you were *sacked* from it. What happened?

RON: I stopped working to listen to 'Music While You Work'. But when I came back and told the Labour Exchange Manager — well, Eth, remarks were passed which I hope you won't ask me to repeat.

ETH: Why not, Ron?

RON: I've forgotten them. But I had to say to the Manager, 'If that's your attitude, Mr Turner, I am going to take my patronage elsewhere. So would you kindly give me my name and address back.'

ETH: (*angry*) And so I should blooming think so! Oh, Ron, I'm sorry to use language — but I think you did quite right. You can find a job without *their* blooming help. The papers advertise hundreds of them every night. Which of the evening papers does your father usually take?

RON: The one under the iron bar. He says you often find pennies on it.

ETH: Well, I bet we'll get you fixed up from there in no time. Show that Mr Turner he can't treat you like a doormat. You know what I've always said, Ron. There's nothing you can't do if you just turn your mind to it.

RON: Right ho, Eth.

ETH: No, Ron, I didn't mean that —

RON: Go on, Eth, it's been weeks —

ETH: No, Ron, not when you've been licking Green Stamps. Ron, this skirt rides *up* —

The door opens and Mr Glum enters, carrying the evening paper.

MR GLUM: Hallo, hallo, hallo. Ron been to see 'Invasion Of The Body Snatchers'? Well, I'm sorry to interrupt but there's something on the telly I'm rather keen on. Ah! (*Picks up bottle of gin from top of TV, makes to exit*)

ETH: Mr Glum, could you possibly stay a sec?

MR GLUM: Sorry, Eth, I'm too busy to stay here for secs. Mrs Glum's gone out for the evening and left me to fill up some registration form for 'all members of the household eligible to vote'. Off hand, Ron, can you remember your mother's Christian name?

ETH: All we really wanted was that evening paper, Mr Glum. For Ron. He's going to make a determined effort to find himself a job.

MR GLUM: No?! Well, good for you, boy! (*Opens the evening paper at appropriate section*) I was only saying to our local candidate last week,

'You'll never be able to say this country's got full employment till you've solved the Ron problem.'

ETH: Any *suitable* positions advertised, Mr Glum?

MR GLUM: Just looking for the column, Eth. Ah, here we are — 'Sits Vacant'. Well, if that's not an apt description of Ron, what is? Right, let's have a butcher's.

ETH: Is there anything you particularly *fancy*, Ron?

RON: Well, I wouldn't mind a banana.

MR GLUM: In the job line! For heaven's sake — hasn't even clocked *on* and already he wants a tea-break! (*Sits down with paper at table*) All right — quickest way to get this done, is do it systematically. I'll call out all the available occupations advertised, you give me your reaction. Right, Ron?

RON: Right, Dad.

MR GLUM: Well — Audit clerk.

RON: No, Dad.

MR GLUM: Bricklayer's mate?

RON: No, Dad.

MR GLUM: Cellulose sprayer?

RON: No, Dad.

MR GLUM: Petrol pump attendant?

RON: No, Dad.

MR GLUM: Stock-room assistant?

RON: No, Dad.

MR GLUM: Tool-and-jig maker?

RON: (*triumphant*) No, Dad!

MR GLUM: (*despair*) Well, I dunno ...

RON: I'll give you a hint. I am non-wage-earning.

ETH: Ron, we're not playing 'What's My Line?'! We're trying to help you place yourself somewhere *congenial*. Look, let's narrow it down — do you want a white-collar job?

RON: ... Like a vicar?

ETH: No, I was thinking of something in an office. On second thoughts, though, do you see Ron stuck over a desk all day, Mr Glum? I think he's more the outdoor type.

MR GLUM: Well, can't we compromise, then? Find a profession which combines totting up of figures with healthy outdoor *exercise* ... I've got it! Bookie's runner!

ETH: Oh, Mr Glum no! Never! I'd rather Ron be unemployed.

Week ending November 17, 1951   EVERY THURSDAY 3½ᴰ

Picturegoer

THE NATIONAL FILM WEEKLY

DORIS DAY

"LULLABY" TEAM
• • •
ROMMEL'S
NEW WAR
• • •
INSIDE THE JOY FACTORY

Mr. Attlee's doctors have advised him to restrict his smoking . . . when he does light up it is with evident pleasure

Thousand Miles From No. 10

Mr. and Mrs. Attlee found holiday delights among Norway's fjords, mountains and valleys

ICE-BLUE arms of the glaciers and glistening, snow-covered mountain peaks, pushed Whitehall and Cabinet meetings into the dim background while Mr. and Mrs. Attlee were the guests of the Norwegian Government.

Their first trip was to the Jotunheimen, Norway's most famous mountain district and the home of the gods of mythology. High up on the roof of Norway, Mrs. Attlee insisted on walking to the nearest glacier and persuaded her husband to accompany her.

She proved to be an expert mountain walker, climbing the stones with ease, nearly always hurrying some 200 yards ahead of the Prime Minister and the rest of the party.

When the distance between them became too far she sat down to wait for her husband to catch up, but a few minutes later she would again be a few hundred yards ahead. She said the mountain air was so invigorating that she could not stop hurrying.

At the glacier, Mrs. Attlee
Continued on page 45

Melting glaciers leave ice-cold pools among the wild landscape on the roof of Norway

Helping hand from host, Mr. A. Elvesaeter

RON: Right ho, Eth. (*Rising*) There you are, Dad, I knew if we kept at it, we'd find something. You give up too easy, Dad, that's your —

MR GLUM: Will you sit down and shut up! Gawd in heaven, trying to get an idea through his head is like trying to housetrain King Kong. It's a job we're trying to find you — and find you one we *will*, if it takes all night. Now pay attention. (*Takes up page again*) Hebrew teacher —

RON: No, Dad.

Music — and we go forward to — The same scene. Four hours later.

MR GLUM: (*wearily*) Piano polisher?

RON: No, Dad.

MR GLUM: Metallurgical chemist?

RON: No, Dad.

MR GLUM: Non-ferrous capstan-head-lathe-turner and buffer?

RON: (*considers*) ... Nnn-no, Dad!

MR GLUM: 'Exchange hardly worn ski-ing boots for invalid chair'? Eh? Oh, lummy, I'm on to the Personal Column now. Eth, we've gone through the complete list. Every single job on offer! And he's just as much a drug on the market as when we started.

ETH: (*defensive*) It's not Ron's fault, Mr Glum. He's been cooperating. It's just — well, look at the time! Who can be enthusiastic about *any* job at twenty past two in the morning?

MR GLUM: (*grave*) Eth, I know Ron. If we give up now, he may not feel like employment again for *ages*. With him, it's a sort of — seven year itch.

ETH: Then why don't we try getting at the problem another way? From Ron's personal angle. Ron, beloved — do you know what you *want* to do?

RON: Yes, Eth.

ETH: Not just vaguely, Ron. Quite *firmly*.

RON: Quite firmly, Eth.

ETH: Well, what *do* you want to do?

RON: I want to go to bed.

MR GLUM: (*angrily*) You can't make a career of that! Well, not in this part of London.

ETH: Mr Glum, losing your paddy's not going to help. I tell you what. Let's try writing down all the things Ron is actually *good* at. Then we'll have an idea the sort of job he's *fitted* for.

MR GLUM: Ah! Now that, at last, sounds like a sensible suggestion. All right (*he fetches pencil and paper*) — write down a nice neat list ... Now — all the things he's good at. Ready?

ETH: (*pencil poised*) Ready.

MR GLUM: One! He can … (*pause*) … He can … (*long pause; scratches head, rubs jaw*)

ETH: Well?

MR GLUM: Let's *all* go to bed.

ETH: (*flare up*) That's exactly the trouble, Mr Glum. Nobody *believes* in Ron. For once in his life he took the bull between the horns and *inserted* himself — but what support does he get? Really, it makes me so boiling. If you want a list of his good qualities, *I'll* give 'em to you.

MR GLUM: (*retreat*) All right, Eth, all right.

ETH: Well — where to begin? He's patient … he's quiet … he doesn't fidget … he's … he's got well-shaped ears … he's patient …

MR GLUM: We've *had* that! (*Irritable*) 'Patient … quiet … well-shaped ears'? We're putting him into *commerce*, not Crufts! May I remind you, Eth, in the cut-and-thrust world of free enterprise competition, you can't *rely* on just immobility and a good pair of harkers. It's a jungle out there.

ETH: But there must be *some* kind of job where they're — wait a minute, Mr Glum! Half a *mo*'! Ron, when I said you never fidget, you really don't, do you?

RON: No, Eth.

ETH: You can sit for hours and *hours* sometimes without one flicker of expression on your face, can't you, beloved?

RON: Yes, Eth. It's a sort of gift.

ETH: (*triumph*) There, Mr Glum! Perhaps you'll now tell me *that's* not in demand!

MR GLUM: (*at sea*) I'm not with you, Eth. Perhaps if you'd vouchsafe some particularisation of —

ETH: I'll do more than that. I'll show you! Never mind *this* paper! (*Gets up, looks around*) Where's the local?

MR GLUM: The local? You going to hire him out as a dartboard?

ETH: The local *paper*! (*Finds it*) Now — (*searches through it*) — if my memory serves me — (*finds what she's been looking for*) — Yes! (*Thrusts paper at Mr Glum*) What about *that*?

MR GLUM: (*reads*) 'MAN WANTED FOR ASSAULT ON CUB-MISTRESS'? Oh, Eth, that's not a *job* offer, it's a —

ETH: *Under* that! Where it advertises the adult evening classes at the Institute. Can't you see what it says *there*?

MR GLUM: Nothing that jumps *out* at me. All it says is — 'Tuesday — Men's Carpentry Class'. 'Wednesday — Ladies' Poetry Group' … (*he looks up*) I still don't —

ETH: Read on. What does it say for *Thursday*?

MR GLUM: (*reads*) 'Thursday — Advanced Water Colour Painting ... Life Class'.

ETH: And in brackets *after* that?

MR GLUM: In brackets, 'Male model required. Five shillings per hour' ... Five ... ? Eth! Eth, I doff my titfer to you, I do really. That's *it*! Ron, you're going to be a model!

RON: A model what?

MR GLUM: A model for painters! 'Patience, quietness, immobility'. You're absolutely right, Eth — he's got the lot!

ETH: All you have to do, Ron, is stand on a plinth while they paint your picture.

RON: Plinth?

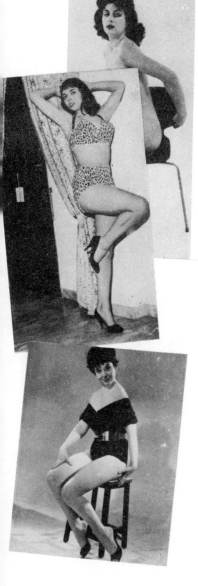

ETH: (*sudden shy-making thought*) Mind you, what you *might* have to do is — ... well, I suppose you'd definitely have to — have to ... well, it does say 'Life Class', Ron.

RON: What's the matter, Eth? Your face has gone the colour of Dad's nose.

MR GLUM: What Eth is implying, Ron, is that — well, it does entail devastating yourself of clothing.

RON: (*horrified*) What clothing, Dad?

MR GLUM: The *lot*, Ron. Shirt, vest, shoes, socks, cornplasters — everything! In other words, you'd be stark naked.

RON: (*terror*) ... Ooh!

ETH: Mind you, it is *Art*, Ron. So it would only be sort of *symbolic*, wouldn't it, Mr Glum?

MR GLUM: Yes, I should have put it like that, Ron. You'd be stark *symbolic* naked.

RON: Ooh, Dad ...

MR GLUM: Ron! Don't come over all booje-war about it. Nothing to be ashamed of. Regarded from the artistic viewpoint, the nude human body is the noblest work of nature.

RON: It's not my body I'm ashamed of, Dad. It's my vest.

MR GLUM: Oh, easy enough to put a few patches on *that*, lad. I've still got some of that rubber solution. The important thing is, Ron — tonight you could be taking the first step to wealth and success.

ETH: That plinth may only be a small start, dearest — but it is something to go *on* from.

RON: (*infected with the enthusiasm*) And I will, Eth! I'll be a better and better artists' model. Don't worry. I'm not going to stand still!

Music, and we return to — the pub, night.

LANDLORD: Well, I reckon that's little short of a brainwave, Mr Glum! Making him an artists' model!

MR GLUM: Well, as so often happens in life, Ted, it's one of those things that's staring you in the face but you just don't *see* it. And though that might not be the best thought to express in connection with a nude model — we certainly got lucky when we sent his particulars to the art class teacher. Had a very nice letter back inviting Ron to start that very week. So I took him outside and gave him a good hose-down in the back-yard — then Eth done his hair in all little *curls*. Like that Greek God — woss-his-name — Useless.

LANDLORD: I always thought he was pronounced Yewly-Sees.

MR GLUM: Translations vary. But two nights later, off he went to the Institute. And you can imagine the impatience with which Eth and me sat waiting for his triumphal return ...

Music, and we go back to the Glums' front room, night.

ETH: Still another three hours, Mr Glum. I only hope I'll be able to stand the strain.

MR GLUM: *I* only hope they've got some heat in that Institute. He's very prone to goose-pimples is Ron. Standing there a whole evening in the altogether — his skin'll wind up looking like corn-on-the-cob.

ETH: I don't think we've got anything to *worry* about, myself. I've never seen Ron so confident.

MR GLUM: Me, neither. That's what worries me.

ETH: Oh, you do like to belittle him, don't you? All he's got to do is undress and stand there. What can possibly —

There's an official-sounding knock at the front door.

MR GLUM: Hallo ... who can that be? (*Getting up and going out*) It's not Ron's knock. He always does 'Dragnet'.

He opens front door. There stands a policeman.

POLICEMAN: Excuse me, sir, is your name Glum?

MR GLUM: Lummy — the law! What is it, Constable? It's Mrs Glum, isn't it? She's had an accident — my dear wife, something happened to her! I had a presentment, I *knew* it — from the moment I found that four-leafed clover —

POLICEMAN: Mr Glum — do you have a son name of Ronald?

MR GLUM: I refuse to answer that question on the grounds I might incriminate myself.

ETH: (*coming to join Mr Glum*) What's happened to him? Where is he?

From behind Policeman, Ron enters — his head all curls, wearing only a raincoat, bare-legged, bare-footed — and handcuffed.

RON: Hallo, Eth.

ETH: (*pointing to his hands*) Ron — why are you —? (*Distraught*) Constable, what's his crime? What's he done?

POLICEMAN: (*consulting noteboong notebook*) Ronald Glum is charged that at two minutes past eight this evening, at the Queens Road Institute, he did divest himself of all clothing, then present himself in front of the Ladies' Poetry Group.

ETH AND MR GLUM: What?

RON: (*anguish*) Dad, today's *Wednesday*!

Playout music and BLACKOUT.

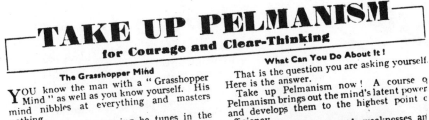

A local Marriage Guidance Bureau, daytime. The telephone on the desk is ringing. It's answered by the counsellor, a handsome, tailored-suit type middle-aged lady.

COUNSELLOR: Hallo, Marriage Guidance Bureau here. Miss Forbes speaking, what is your problem? (*Voice changes, drops*) Look, I told you not to phone me at the office! ... No, I can't now, I have a client. I'll see you at the usual place. (*Puts phone down*) I'm sorry about that interruption, sir.

We now see Mr Glum at opposite side of desk. Dejected.

COUNSELLOR: (*pulling a pad towards her*) Now what did you say your name was?

MR GLUM: Glum. Mr Glum. I meant to get here earlier but I been worrying about this matter so much, I was suddenly taken drunk.

COUNSELLOR: (*sympathetic*) Why don't we talk it through then, Mr Glum? You're consulting us, I presume, about a marital problem?

MR GLUM: Well, partly that — but mostly 'cos I'm having trouble with the missus. I still can't believe she's done this to me! After all this *time*! We been together thirty years, man and beast — and *now*, Miss Forbes, now —

COUNSELLOR: Easy, Mr Glum. Let's see if we can piece the story together from the beginning. (*Making a note*) You say you've been married thirty years?

MR GLUM: Thirty years come next St Leger.

COUNSELLOR: And was the marriage blessed with a child?

MR GLUM: No. All we had was Ron. He's my son. He's sort of — well, how can I describe him? Look, you know how some people do fancy-work?

COUNSELLOR: Yes?

MR GLUM: Well, he *doesn't* fancy work. What's more, he's engaged to this fiancée called Eth.

COUNSELLOR: (*frowns — then*) Eth is presumably a diminutive.

MR GLUM: Well, in *some* areas perhaps — but looks aren't everything, are they? Specially when you remember it was her who found out about the whole tragic business. Three weeks ago, it was — while her and Ron was tangled up together on our front room sofa ...

Music, and we hark back to the Glums' sitting-room, night.

Ron and Eth are on the sofa. The lights are off. They are lit only by the glow of the fire.

ETH: Oh, Ron ... isn't it cosy with just the firelight? No need to talk somehow — it's so nice just being quiet. You been having a little zizz, beloved?

RON: No, Eth.

ETH: What you been doing then?

RON: I been trying to think of something to think about.

ETH: (*sigh*) I'm afraid all I've been thinking about is your mother. At tea-time, Ron, she was so — well, abrupt. Didn't even open her mouth. Just sat glaring at your father, with her lips pressed all tight together. What could Mr Glum have done to make her behave like *that*?

RON: He pawned her teeth.

ETH: (*sitting up*) He — ! Her *teeth*! Well, no wonder she had the hump. Oh, Ron, why doesn't she ever assert herself? If I'd been her, there'd have been a proper set-to.

RON: It was set *two* he pawned, Eth. Her first set went to pay for Christmas.

ETH: I mean no disrespect to your father, Ron, but that woman's a saint to put up with him.

RON: Oh, never mind them, Eth. Put your head back on my shoulder again.

ETH: Why?

RON: (*softly*) I've just thought of something to think about.

ETH: No, not now, Ron. You've got to be in the mood.

RON: I am, Eth. I'm *always* —

ETH: I mean, I couldn't, Ron. Not with the thought of your mother's teeth still fresh in my mind. Put the light on again, there's a pet.

Ron unenthusiastically gets up and goes towards light-switch.

ETH: If your father comes in and finds us in the dark — well, you know him and his insinuendoes.

Ron switches on light.

ETH: (*tasting her lips*) Oh, that fire's made my kissprufe go all crinkled. (*Brings out lipstick*) *You* better run a comb through your hair as well, dearest.

RON: Rightho, Eth. (*Goes to mirror; as he combs he sings to himself:*) 'Chelsea bun, Oh, they do it in France, Yes, they —' (*pause*) — Eth.

ETH: (*lipsticking*) Yes, beloved?

RON: How long have I had a sheet of paper stuck to my forehead?

ETH: A sheet — ? (*Looks up*) Ron, that's stuck on the *mirror*.

RON: Oh.

ETH: (*curious*) Looks like with a piece of chewing-gum. Well, that's odd. What is it, Ron?

RON: (*sniffing it*) ... I think it's Juicy Fruit.

ETH: The piece of paper. Bring it over.

Ron brings her the sheet of paper.

ETH: Some sort of letter, I — (*Scans it, then, chilled*) … Oh, Ron! Oh, she *can't* have! Ron, it's from your mother. She's — (*Bites lip*) — Oh, Ron, do you know *why* she stuck this letter on your mirror with chewing-gum?

RON: To stop it falling off?

ETH: Ron, she's — she's … oh, I can't say it! (*Urgent shout*) Mr Glum! Mr Glum! Please! Come here!

MR GLUM: (*off*) Coming, Eth.

ETH: (*shrill*) Oh, quickly, come *quickly*! Quickly!

The door opens and Mr Glum, clad only in a towel, pelts in at the run, straight at Ron. As he enters —

MR GLUM: I knew this would happen one day! (*The rest of his speech is accompanied by wallops at Ron and Ron's yelping protests*) I've *told* you to leave her be! No self-control, have you? Pleasure-*mad*! Dirty little —

RON: (*simultaneously*) No, Dad, don't, Dad!

MR GLUM: This is a decent house. I'm not having that kind of —

ETH: (*stopping him*) Mr Glum — no! Let Ron be! It's nothing to do with *him*!

MR GLUM: Eh? Then why'd you scream for me like that for? Scared the life out of me. There I was having an all-over wash in the kitchen — you hardly give me time to get my leg out the sink. Could have ricked something and never smiled again.

ETH: Mr Glum, if it wasn't vitally urgent, I'd never have — look at this note we found stuck to the mirror.

MR GLUM: Show me. Oh, blast. Left me glasses on the draining board. (*Becomes conscious of towel round him*) Oh, just look at me! (*Declaims*) 'I come not to bury Caesar, but to praise him, that is the question!'

ETH: Oh, Mr Glum, this is no time for striking larking-about postures. (*Going to sideboard*) Don't you keep some spare glasses in the fruit bowl? (*Thrusts them at him*) Now, for heaven's sake, read.

MR GLUM: (*putting glasses on*) All right, all right. Hallo, I recognize that uncouth handwriting — Mrs Glum, isn't it? Places she leaves her shopping-lists! What's *this* one? (*Reads*) 'This is to inform you I have stood as much as flesh and blood can swallow. I have put both my belongings in that brown paper carrier-bag wot you give me for Christmas … (*slowly*) … and I have left you.' … *Left* me! (*Stricken*) Eth!

ETH: Sit down, Mr Glum. Oh, Ron, look at your father. (*Mr Glum is swaying*) He's pale.

RON: I'll go and fetch it.

ETH: No, sit him down. It's shock. Just take deep breaths, Mr Glum. Ron — you read the rest of the letter.

RON: Right ho, Eth. (*He reads —*)

MR GLUM: Aloud! Read it *aloud*! Blind O'Reilly, I'm not a mental telegraphist!

RON: Oh. It goes on — 'The last ember of the love that glowed between us died the day you pawned my teeth.'

ETH: (*sob*)

RON: 'I see you now for what you are — a loud-mouthed, bullying, no-good toe-rag.'

MR GLUM: (*his face contorts in grief*)

RON: (*stuck for something to say*) ... She writes a nice letter, doesn't she?

ETH: (*disapproving shake of the head*) Ron! (*Gesture of reproof*)

MR GLUM: My wife's left me! (*Helplessly*) Eth, I can't *believe* it, I can't — it's not true, is it?

ETH: (*awkwardly*) These things happen, Mr Glum.

MR GLUM: No. Eth, no! They don't. Not to people like *us*, Eth. You only get it among the *lower* classes.

ETH: I did think she seemed a bit — discontented.

MR GLUM: Discontented? Oh, what errant nonsense! We was hydraulically happy. I gave her everything, everything! Name me one thing she went short of.

ETH: Well — food. Clothes. Coal ... Teeth.

MR GLUM: Who's talking about the luxuries? I mean things that *matter* Companionship! Stimulating conversation! I can't understand it, can't seem to — (*Gestures*)

Alma Cogan's fabulous wardrobe — aided by her personal appeal—won her a leading place in the TV charm parade

ETH: Are you really telling me you're — surprised?

MR GLUM: Surprised … Shocked … Numbed? I don't know. I don't really know *what* I am.

RON: (*indicating letter*) Says here you're a loud-mouthed, bullying, no-good toe —

ETH: Ron!

MR GLUM: What could have made her do this thing? Thirty years, Eth … Funny thing is, I — I can't conjure up her *face* — I mean, her face as it is *now*. Only — only what she looked like — *then*. Just after we'd got engaged. Wearing that *hat* I bought her. Oh, Eth, you'd have loved that hat. Two little feathers — and a lot of big coloured flowers —

ETH: (*softly*) You gave it to her?

MR GLUM: (*nods; lost in past*) I gave it to her. I remember I got it cheap becos it fell off the stall and a dog did something on it. And *now* —? Why, *why*? 'Ere — do you think there's a *man* in it? No, there couldn't be another man. I've just *remembered* what she looks like. Well, I tell you this. I'm not having her *back*!

ETH: But —

MR GLUM: Not if she crawls on her hands and knees! As she's buttered her bread, so she must lie on it. Ron — Ron, my little son … from now on it's just you and me. Do you — do you *mind*?

RON: No, Dad.

MR GLUM: That's my big boy.

RON: There's — there's just *one* thing I feel I should say, Dad.

The Panel Game, which television has made its own, typified in this memory of a happy moment in "What's My Line?" with David Nixon, Isobel Barnett, Barbara Kelly and Gilbert Harding

"Teazy-weazy"

MR GLUM: Yes, Ron?

RON: Not so much as regards you and me — more because of Eth, really.

MR GLUM: Then say it, son, What's troubling you?

RON: (*indicating*) Your towel's slipped.

MR GLUM: Oh, cor lummy … !

As he hastily adjusts, music, and we return to the Marriage Guidance Bureau, day.

The counsellor is shaking her head sympathetically.

COUNSELLOR: We get so many cases like this. But our first concern, Mr Glum, has to be for the child. Is he — *missing* his mother?

MR GLUM: Oh, in so many *little* ways. Like, at *bath*-time. It's pitiful to see him trying to scrub his own back. He's ruined that broom.

COUNSELLOR: And how are *you* coping with running the home?

MR GLUM: I tell you, frankly, Miss Forbes, it's not been easy. Not only do I have all the responsibility of Ron — making sure he puts on his warm pullover and heaviest boots — he's only got thin blankets on his bed — but I've also had to see to all the cooking and *housework* …

Music, and we return to the Glums' sitting-room, daytime.

It's now a shambles: uncleaned plates piled up; dirty laundry everywhere. Ron is sitting dispiritedly as Mr Glum, wearing an apron, bustles in with a steaming plate.

MR GLUM: Here we are, Ron — don't they smell good? Eat 'em while they're nice and hot.

RON: Oh, Dad, no — not again. Dad, we've had nothing else for three weeks now. Breakfast, dinner, tea and supper — baked beans on toast.

MR GLUM: Well, this is a *change*! (*Showing him plate*) See?

RON: What is it?

MR GLUM: Toast on baked beans. I dropped 'em. Now don't go pulling that face.

RON: I don't fancy 'em, Dad.

MR GLUM: (*distracted housewife*) There's me slaving over a hot stove and what do I get? Not so much as a thank you. It's all very well for you, but I've only got one pair of hands and you're no help at all. Why do you have to spend all your time sitting in the coal-hole?

RON: It's *cleaner* in there.

MR GLUM: I'll get *round* to the dusting. I've got a thousand other things to — (*indicating*) — there's still all that washing waiting to be done. Shirts, vests, socks — I don't know why them blooming commercials keep going on about 'whiter than white'. What they *ought* to come out with is a detergent that folds and *irons*!

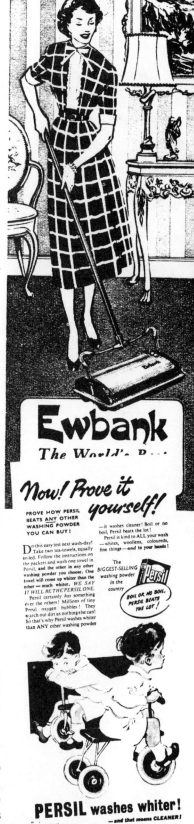

ETH: (outside) Yoo-hoo!

MR GLUM: Now there's Eth! (Calls) Just a minute, my dear. (Pulls motor bike away from door) Just let me give you room to — there! (As Eth squeezes in) Sorry if there seems a bit of a mess, but you're seeing the room under the worst possible conditions. Daylight.

ETH: (looking round, incredulous) I'd never have believed a place could get in such a condition.

RON: You should have seen it before I tidied up.

ETH: Mr Glum, this room is not fit for human habitation to live in! And — (Wrinkling her nose) — What's that? (Sniffing distastefully) Pew!

MR GLUM: (irritably) You can sniff all you like, Eth, but I got too many things to do to go running out to the dustbin every minute. So I did the one sensible thing women never think of doing.

ETH: Eh?

MR GLUM: (pointing) I brought the dustbin in here.

Following the direction of Mr Glum's finger, Eth sees the dustbin. Ron is desultorily picking unspeakable-looking things from it.

MR GLUM: Ron, what you poking around in it for?

RON: (plaintive) I'm hungry.

ETH: Mr Glum, you can't go on living like this. There'll be a complaint from the Health Prevention Officer.

RON: Please let's get Mum back, Dad. Please. I been hungry for three weeks.

ETH: Mr Glum, how can you let your only child plead like that? Ron, dearest, you miss your mother's cooking, don't you?

RON: It's not just her cooking, Eth. It's her being here. Her voice. Her smile.

MR GLUM: Well, you can see her smile any time you want. Just run down to the pawnbroker's. Oh, Eth, I — (wiping his hands on his apron) — I don't know what to do.

ETH: You've had a change of heart haven't you, Mr Glum?

MR GLUM: It's about all I have had a change of. (Indicating washing all around room). Unless I can get round to some of them soon, the ones we're wearing will go luminous. Oh, Eth — even if I were to want her back — how could I go about it?

ETH: Mr Glum, do you think I haven't been making enquiries about that? And you know what I discovered? There are organisations who specialize in bringing people like Mrs Glum back.

MR GLUM: You mean — haulage contractors?

ETH: Mr Glum, there's a place called — The Marriage Guidance Bureau!

Music, and back we go to the Marriage Guidance Bureau, day.

MR GLUM: So there you have the general situation thus far, Miss Forbes. And that's without even mentioning the state the *kitchen's* in. (*Shudders*) It's like Pompeii in there. So what do you advise?

COUNSELLOR: Frankly, Mr Glum — something I don't think you're going to like. But I honestly can't think of any other way to persuade Mrs Glum to alter her opinion of you.

MR GLUM: Oh, surely we don't have to do nothing *too* drastic. I mean, isn't changing her mind supposed to be a woman's purgative?

COUNSELLOR: (*shaking her head*) In this case, not without some definite inducement. (*Warningly*) And the only inducement I can see working with *her* — will entail quite a *sacrifice* on your part.

MR GLUM: (*sigh*) All right. What do you want me to do?

Music, and over to the Glums' sitting-room, two days later.

Now tidied up again. Mr Glum and Ron are at the table eating. Eth, in her coat, is wandering round the room, delightedly.

ETH: Oh, Mr Glum, she's worked miracles. You must both be so happy. Do you know these curtains are so *clean* I went right past the house. Oh, Mr Glum, I don't know what you did to win Mrs Glum back again — but it must have been something really *romantic*. Don't you agree, Ron?

RON: Yes, Eth.

ETH: But you still haven't told us. I know, you got her teeth *back* from the pawnbrokers — but how did you raise the money for them?

For the first time we see Mr Glum from the front.

MR GLUM: (*toothless*) I should have thought that was perfectly obvious. Now hurry up and mix me some more bread-and-milk.

As he gummily tucks in, playout music and BLACKOUT.

THE JOB INTERVIEW

Scruffy hair?
Girls hate it!

End **Dry Scalp**
and notice the difference

Oh-oh-Dry Scalp!

Can't miss it, can you? That dry lifeless, *scruffy* look, or maybe flakes of dandruff in the parting and on the collar. It all shouts "Dry Scalp" loud and clear!

Girls hate 'scruffy' ... or flecke... Dry Scalp—...

All you ne... 'Vaseline' Bra... moving the wh... and dressing v...

Your hair w... better. And rem... economical at 2,...

Tenova REGD.
socks
stay up

THE COMFORT'S
IN THE CUT-OUT

From ... all go...

What a difference 'Vaseline' Hair Tonic makes! Your hair looks much better and your scalp *feels* much better when you call in that crystal-clear hair ... Get a bottle ...

The pub, night. Pub hubbub, over which:

LANDLORD: *(shouting)* Drink up, gents. Your last orders, please. Time, gentlemen. Here, Mr Glum, I saw your boy Ron yesterday and — tell you the truth — I hardly recognized him. Smart brown suit, new shoes, trilby — where'd he get them? How much they cost you? Where'd you find the money?

MR GLUM: Cor lummy, Ted — you ask more questions than the Spanish Imposition. As perchance would have it, that whole get-up of Ron's did not cost us a penny.

LANDLORD: You got that entire outfit for *free*?

MR GLUM: Absolutely au gratin.

LANDLORD: You're pulling my leg!

MR GLUM: I wouldn't lower myself. It is absolute fact. And if you want to know the reason why he *needed* them clothes, it was because — well, if you'll secrete another brown in this receptacle I'll go back to last Sunday night. 'Cos that was when his fiancée Eth first raised the subject in question ...

Music, and we hark back to the Glums' sitting-room, night.

Ron is looking more than usually down-at-heel. Eth is animated.

ETH: Oh, Ron — you are a *devil* sometimes! I *knew* you had a surprise for me as soon as I came in tonight. Moment I set eyes on you, I thought — 'My Ron's got a little twinkle' ... Was I wrong, beloved?

RON: No, Eth.

ETH: Talk about a deep one! Right in the middle of a Montpelier drop, you turn round and announce that tomorrow afternoon you're going for a *job* interview! *(Teasingly tweaking his nose)* My business man! Let me look at you. *(She sits up and looks at him, smiling fondly; then the smile fades)* Ron — are you going for the interview like *that*?

RON: Like what, Eth?

ETH: Exactly as you are now?

RON: Oh, no, Eth. By three o'clock tomorrow I'll have *finished* the Montpelier drop.

ETH: I was really referring to — well, what I'm a little bit *worried* about, Ron, is — to be quite frank — your get-up.

RON: Oh, you don't have to worry about that, Eth. I'll borrow the alarm-clock.

ETH: Your clothes, Ron! If you can go to an interview looking neat and presentable, it's half the battle, beloved. They do put an awful lot of store by appearances.

RON: Is there something wrong with my appearances, Eth?

ETH: Well, beloved — well, to start with — that shirt.

RON: That was Dad's Christmas present, Eth. It's one of the new sort. (*Proudly*) You don't have to *iron* it.

ETH: (*gently*) But, beloved — that doesn't mean you don't have to *wash* it. Oh, I know it's not easy for you, Ron, but well, you really should try and smarten up before that interview. I don't mean be flash. Just — suitable. I mean — well, are those the only shoes you've got?

RON: Yes, Eth, I did have a brown and white pair. But I seem to have lost the brown one.

ETH: (*troubled*) If you really want the truth, Ron, I would say you're wrong all the way up. Even your cap. These days they're wearing them *flat*. Whereas yours is all bulgy.

RON: Is it, Eth? I can't see it very well from down here.

ETH: There's really only one thing for it, Ron. If you want to *pass* this interview, your father's got to buy you a complete new outfit. Do you think he'll do it, beloved? Be about twenty pounds.

RON: Well, Eth, Dad knows how important this interview is for me and if there's one thing my father does care about it's my future, especially when it — (*pause; then*) — HOW MUCH?

ETH: Twenty pounds.

RON: No, Eth.

ETH: Then we've somehow got to *make* him, Ron. He's got to be ... what's the word I'm looking for? — 'goaded'!

RON: Oh, no, Eth. I don't think there's such a word as 'goaded'. One says '*went*'.

ETH: There are occasions, Ron, when I think you're just *too* placid. This is one time when I wish you'd have a little *go*!

RON: Right ho, Eth.

ETH: No, Ron, I didn't mean that — not during 'What's My Line' —

RON: Go on, Eth, just a kiss —

ETH: Ron, Lady Barnett's looking straight *at* us — No —

The door opens and Mr Glum enters.

MR GLUM: 'Allo, 'allo, 'allo! My, my, Ron — I can see we'll have to switch you back to white bread. (*Chuckle*) ... Well, I won't interrupt, I just came in for a bottle of ink and the slop-pail. Mrs Glum's going to give herself a blue rinse.

ETH: No, Mr Glum, don't go. Have you heard about Ron's job interview tomorrow?

MR GLUM: What do you *think* of that, eh, Eth? At last my boy's got his teeth on the first rung of the ladder! They called him a layabout — but I *knew*, Eth. I knew he was just biding his time. It's like his Uncle Charlie once said — 'Never settle for the *first* thing that catches your eye. Always try out a lot of *different* opportunities before making up your mind.'

RON: When did he say that, Dad?

MR GLUM: Just before they nicked him for bigamy ... Wossmore, Eth, if you're nervous about him passing that interview, he'll pass hands down. You know why because? Because it's a *challenge*! And that's what Ron *rises* to. His talents are always *there* — but most of the time they're lying doormat. Comes a challenge — and *ah*! His true worth rises to the surface like — like a corn-plaster when you're having a bath.

ETH: Well, I do hope so, of course ...

MR GLUM: No 'hope' about it. Is there, Ron?

RON: No, Dad, No hope at all.

MR GLUM: The reason I say that so confidently, Eth, is because that's how *I* am. And he's got very like me has my Ron. You know why he's become so like me?

ETH: Yes, Mr Glum. (*Pointed*) Because he has to wear your old clothes.

MR GLUM: (*startled*) I beg your pardon, Eth. There's no call to take a degoratory tone about them jacket and trousers. If they were good enough for my father ...

ETH: Now, don't take offence, Mr Glum. All I'm saying is, these clothes are going to spoil Ron's *chances* tomorrow. I mean, just look at them.

MR GLUM: What's wrong with them? I admit there's a few egg-stains on the lapel ... and a bit of soup on the tie ... and come to that, his pullover ain't exactly lacking in calories either, Though he may not be *smart*, Eth — you got to admit he's nourishing. (*Chuckle*)

ETH: It's all very well you treating it lightly, Mr Glum — but if Ron goes for a job looking like that, he will not stand one earthly.

MR GLUM: Oh, come now, Eth. I find that hard to credulate.

ETH: Mr Glum, *believe* me. I know about employers — much more so than any of your family, because — well, because I've actually had *employment*. Do you know the first thing they always look for?

RON: The brown ale?

ETH: Not your family, Ron. Potential employers. They look for how a person is dressed. I mean, doesn't it stand to reason?

MR GLUM: (*grudging*) Well — yes. Yes, I suppose it does. After all, they do say, don't they, 'Clothes maketh the man'?

RON: And not just Eth, Dad. Me as well.

MR GLUM: Now, Ron, don't irate me. She's set me a problem here. Well, all right, Eth — if it's just a question of re-*equipping* him for tomorrow, I don't mind splashing out a bit. After all, I still got thirty bob left of Mrs Glum's burial money.

ETH: Thirty bob? Mr Glum, to dress Ron really befitting, you'll have to spend at least — twenty pounds.

MR GLUM: Twenty —?! Oh, it's out of the question. I've had very heavy back-payment of tax to pay. Ever since the Revenue found I've been

BAD SKIN COST HIM HIS JOB

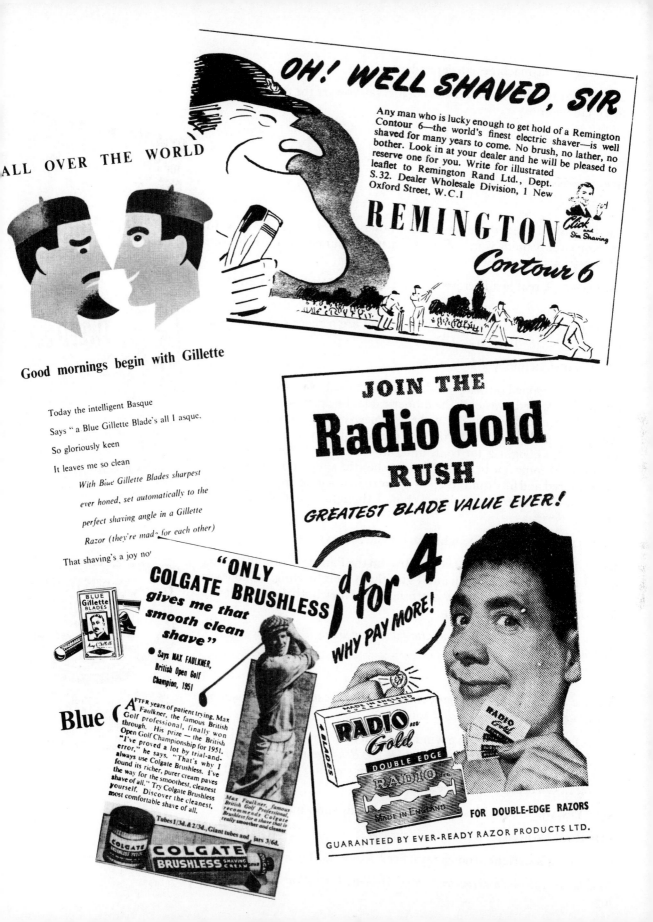

claiming a fruit-machine as a dependent relative.

ETH: Mr Glum, did you or did you not just say you are the type who rises to a challenge?

MR GLUM: Well — yes.

ETH: Well, this is a challenge. So go on then — *rise*!

Music, and we return to the pub, night.

MR GLUM Well, Ted, there was a right poser of a problem, eh? How to get Ron twenty quids worth of gents' natty without having the requisite wherewithal to pay for it thereof.

LANDLORD: A real head-scratcher, I'd call that. I'd say it was impossible.

MR GLUM: Which, Ted, is exactly why you are a mere servant of the brewery while *I* am ... (*modestly*)

LANDLORD: Unemployed?

MR GLUM: A valued *customer*! And where I suddenly saw the solution of our problem, Ted, was over the dinner-table. Because what we always have over the dinner-table is a sheet of newspaper. And while I was reading *my* end — I come across this paragraph. It was a case about a woman who bought a fur coat, and, after wearing it some time, she found she'd come out in a rash! So she sues the shop and they paid up two hundred and fifty quid. Well — as you can imagine, my fertile mind immediately started fertilizing. What, I thought, what about Ron's drip-dry *shirt*?

LANDLORD: The one you bought him for Christmas?

MR GLUM: (*agreeing*) From Loveday Bros on the Parade. Without further ado, I called in Eth and Ron and I give them their briefing. Which was why, Ted, first thing Monday morning, there they both were at Messrs Loveday Bros' shirt counter ...

Music and off we go to the shirt department of a suburban 1950s men's outfitters, daytime.

Ron and Eth are waiting at counter. Eth is clutching the shirt Ron was wearing. Ron's face is covered in unconvincing spots.

ETH: Oh, Ron, I've got such a wind up about this. If it wasn't your whole future's at stake, I'd never even have — (*As Ron fingers a spot, she drops her voice to an urgent whisper*) — Oh, Ron, you keep *touching* those, they'll just rub off ... Oh dear, where's the shop-man?

RON: Yes, where's the blasted, perishing, ruddy shop-man?

ETH: Ron! No need for that kind of *language*.

RON: Eth, it's all right to nowadays. See? 'Modern Men Swear'.

He indicates a placard near counter. It says 'Modern Men's Wear'.

ETH: No, Ron, that says — careful, now!

The warning is occasioned by the entrance of an assistant.

ASSISTANT: Good morning, madam, sir. Can I be of any help?

ETH: Are you one of the Mr Lovedays?

ASSISTANT: Yes, madam.

ETH: Well, I have a complaint.

RON: No, Eth, *I've* got the complaint — these spots on my face. Don't you remember Dad explaining while he was putting them on with the —

ETH: (*sotto*) Ron! Your father said to leave *me* to do the talking. (*Up*) Mr Loveday, I wish to complain that this drip-dry shirt purchased from your establishment has brought my fiancé's face out.

ASSISTANT: Oh, no, madam, it couldn't have done. Whatever caused those curious marks on the gentleman's face, I'm quite sure it wasn't one of our shirts. That's quite out of the —

Mr Glum, who's been lurking nearby, comes forward. He's dressed in an attempt at grandeur.

MR GLUM: Pardon me, I couldn't help but overhearing this conversation. I wonder if I may be of any help?

ASSISTANT: Help?

MR GLUM: It so happens, I happen to be a highly-respected Harley Street medical skin specialist. So if you need an impartial adjudicator in this bull-and-cow —?

RON: Oh yes, please, Dad.

ASSISTANT: *Dad*?

MR GLUM: (*hasty chuckle*) Young man's recognized me, eh? Penalty of fame. (*Proferring a hand*) Doctor Eustace Dadd. Often been in the newspapers for my uncanny diagnostics. May I inspect this lad's outbreak? (*Peering at Ron's spots*) Oh yes ... yes! Tell me, lad, did you at any time — this is just a chance in a million, mind you — but did you at any time happen to wear a drip-dry shirt next to your skin?

RON: No.

MR GLUM: No?

RON: It was next to my pullover.

MR GLUM: I didn't mean reading from outside *in*! I mean working from your body out towards the fresh air?

RON: Oh yes, I did. That shirt I had for Christmas.

MR GLUM: As I thought. (*Gravely*) Mr Loveday, I'm afraid this rash is an absolute classic case of dripdrymatitis. Classic! I shall probably write it up for my next article in the Lancelot.

ASSISTANT: Now just a minute, Doctor. That can't be! We've sold hundreds of these shirts.

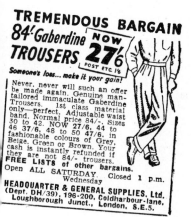

23 August, 1952

PICTURE POST

NOW **4**D AGAIN

HULTON'S NATIONAL WEEKLY

FOOTBALL AGAIN! **4**D

23 AUGUST 1952 VOL 56 • NO 8

MR GLUM: Are you venturing to doubt my professional velocity? Because I warn you, Mr Loveday — though I may be a skin specialist, I am not given to rash statements.

ASSISTANT: And I'm not given to being hoodwinked. If you want my opinion, these spots look like dabs of nail-varnish!

MR GLUM: What a heartless incineration! If that's to be your attitude, sir, then I have to inform you that although my professional services are not usually available to such National Health herberts as these two — I will go into any witness-box and swear on a stack of Bibles them spots are *not* nail-varnish.

RON: They're red ink.

MR GLUM: (*to Eth, heated*) Will you tell your spotty friend to close his yap? Mr Loveday, speaking as one member of the monied classes to another, my expert advice would be to reimburse this unfortunate couple for the agonizing suffering your shirtery has inflicted. Twenty nicker ought to do it.

ASSISTANT: Twenty —!

MR GLUM: Or tell you what — *goods* to the value thereof might be a sort of superior equivalent. New suit ... shoes ... tie ... smart trilby —

RON: Don't forget the nice drip-dry shirt.

ETH: Ron!

RON: Well, I've always found them very good, Eth.

ASSISTANT: (*points at Ron*) This is nothing less than a put-up blackmail job!

MR GLUM: Well, please yourself. If you want to fight it through the courts, it's up to you. Make good reading in the local paper though, won't it? 'Local Outfitter Starts Plague'.

ASSISTANT: (*furious*) Very well, take the blasted things. Take them and get out! Just get out of my shop and stay out!

As trio separate to pick up items of clothing, music, and we return to the Glums' sitting-room, an hour later.

Just Mr Glum and Eth. Eth looks at clock, anxious.

ETH: If he's not dressed soon, he's going to be late. (*Goes to door, pauses*) You know, Mr Glum, I'm still in two minds about what we did. (*Worried*) It does seem a kind of — stealing.

MR GLUM: All I would say, Eth, is — needs must when the devil drives. You can't make an omelette without breaking eggs.

ETH: (*brightening*) Yes, that's true. (*She leaves*)

MR GLUM: (*thoughtfully gazing after her; to himself*) I bet you could get her to do *anything* as long as there's a proverb covering it. (*Looks at clock, calls*) Ron — it's nearly quarter to!

Sunday Dispatch
FOUNDED 1801
MANCHESTER: NORTHCLIFFE HOUSE BLACKFRIARS 8600
EDINBURGH: FREDERICK STREET EDINBURGH CENTRAL 2525
LONDON: NORTHCLIFFE HOUSE. CENTRAL 6000.
MARCH 29, 1953

'GRANDMA ENGLAND'

WHEN the young Queen who is soon to be enthroned was a little girl, one of the happiest stories that came from her nursery was this:

Her infant mind was grappling with the problem that has taxed many other young minds. Does "Grandpa" mean mother's father? Or does it mean father's father? Or, if it means both, how do you tell people what you are really trying to say?

So, vaguely grasping the material of her early introductions to history, she coined for King George V. the resounding title of "Grandpa England."

This week-end it is "Grandma England" on whom our thoughts are centred. For with the passing of Queen Mary something has gone from the life of the nation that for long cannot be replaced.

Men Who Follow

Today will set in history the last of the great ceremonial processions in which Queen Mary has figured.

From her home she will be carried to Westminster Hall. Behind the coffin will walk four men—the Duke of Edinburgh, the Duke of Gloucester, the young Duke of Kent, and the Duke of Windsor.

One the consort of the young granddaughter who is now Queen; one a son who has shared unbrokenly with Queen Mary the splendour and the griefs of the Royal Family; one the son himself of a son who was killed in the war; and finally the son who was to have been crowned.

Over the procession today, and the lying-in-state tomorrow, lies even more than the usual sombre drama of royal death.

Queen Mary takes with her into eternity the private anguished thoughts of a mother whose sons were involved in a story that will surely live in legend—the Abdication of an Empire Throne.

One of the dominant figures in that historic episode has preceded her to the tomb. The other walks behind her today.

As the procession with all its mournful panoply moves through London the thoughts of all will be with the wife and mother whose private emotions were of necessity subordinated to the clear if sometimes harsh call of public duty.

Her courage in grief and her dignified composure at all times leave us with an indelible picture of her in our minds.

Her Contribution

Queen Mary in her 85 years saw much sadness, but she shared in much compensating rejoicing and glory.

It is saddening that she was not able to stay among us to witness and to rejoice in the event shortly ahead when our new Queen Elizabeth will dedicate herself to the service of her people as did her father and grandfather before her.

But Queen Mary has died secure in the knowled… that never have the peoples of Britain … monwealth been so bound i… Throne.

To that bo…

She has live… loyal sympathy … the members of t…

And to the m… love and gratitude…

Queen Mary Bequeaths To Us A Rainbow Bridge With The Past

THE END OF AN ERA

By Sir Compton Mackenzie

AS the passing bell tolled over the air just before midnight on Tuesday, March 24, it seemed to the present writer, as it must have seemed to all his contemporaries who were listening to the solemn sound, that with the spirit of our venerated and beloved Queen Mary an epoch was passing, too.

The great-granddaughter of George III. and the great-grandmother of the Heir Apparent, she, who until a few days ago was the living embodiment of two momentous centuries of monarchy, is no longer with us.

1953

1867

When Queen Mary was born in 1867 work had started on the District Railway at Westminster (left). In 1953 it was the era of delta-wing aircraft. . . .

Called Princess May

It was a minute before midnight on May 26, 1867, when, in the room in Kensington Palace which 40 years earlier had been the nursery of Queen Victoria, Princess Mary Adelaide of Teck brought into this world the infant Princess who would be christened Princess Victoria Mary Augustine Louise Olga Pauline Claudine Agnes, but known for the first 25 years of her life as Princess May.

Hardly a week before her birth Queen Victoria, with a golden trowel, had laid the foundation stone of the Royal Albert Hall, the walls of which were rising during her early childhood. We can scarcely imagine Kensington without the Albert Hall; it is even more difficult to imagine London without Queen Mary.

The Duke and Duchess of Teck were often financially embarrassed in those early years, one cause of that embarrassment being the generosity of the Duchess, who for so long was the best loved of all the Royal Family, particularly by the people of London.

Artistic

IN 1883, when Princess Mary was 16, the Tecks went to recuperate financially in Florence, and the impact made upon that young Princess's imagination by Italy was to bear fruit in an artistic taste which had not manifested itself in the Royal House since her great-great-uncle, George IV. The interior of Buckingham Palace today is a monument to that good taste coupled with the knowledge and experience of a connoisseur.

Princess May was a high-spirited girl with a lively sense of humour; an old Chamberlain of the Württemberg Court at Stüttgart once recalled to the present writer those high spirits. She would hide behind a pillar at a Court Ball and trip up some functionary as he went by, or she would suddenly cause confusion in a quadrille by pushing some stately performer in the back.

S… Of Fun

…EEN MARY'S …andfather, Duke …exander, was …d he may have …omething of his …ungarian bride, …dine Rhédey, … so tragically …rom her horse …iew in Vienna

… fun, though it had to be displayed less boisterously in the exalted position she was to fill with such regal perfection, never left Queen Mary throughout her long life.

That Queen Victoria should have recognised in Princess May of Teck the ideal Queen Consort of the future demands a tribute to her judgment. Princess May's engagement to the Duke of Clarence was announced in that bleak December of 1891. A month later the Duke died, and his brother, the Duke of York, stepped into the direct line of succession.

It was now Queen Victoria's ardent hope that Princess May should become the bride of her favourite grandson, and so on a glorious July day 60 years ago, in that azure summer of 1893, the Duke and Duchess of York were married in the Chapel Royal, St. James's, and the crowds cheered them all the way to Liverpool Street on the way to their honeymoon at Sandringham.

A Legend

THE young Duchess of York was intellectually much more advanced than the inner circle of Royalty into which she had married, and during those 18 years before she became Queen she imposed upon herself the most rigid discipline, so rigid indeed that the memory of her high-spirited youth vanished from peo… legend gre… husband … were dull.

As Prir… was credi… tion of r… of the C… came Qu… the Victo…

To sor… to say … Wales d… figure beside that of his father, but the Prince of Wales had a strength of character which was not in the least realised outside of the very small circle of his intimate friends, and Queen Mary herself never made the mistake of supposing that she was able to influence him in the way that Queen Alexandra could and did influence King Edward VII.

'A Comfort'

WHAT Queen Mary did for George V. was to give him continuous support. When he wrote in his diary on the evening of their Coronation: "*Darling May looked so lovely and it was indeed a comfort to me to have her by my side as she has been ever to me during those last 18 years,*" he wrote from the depths of his heart.

King George ascended the throne almost with perturbation about his ability to take his father's place; what he must have owed to Queen Mary's confidence in him was a debt of which he was conscious and for which he was grateful for the rest of his days.

It is improbable that King George and Queen Mary were fully aware of the extent of the social revolution that the First World War would precipitate, but without doubt from the moment that they became King and Queen they … the need of … burdens never laid upon it before.

We talk glibly enough of the tremendous changes that the 20th century has brought about, but how many of us stop to consider the astonishing serenity, dignity, and vitality with which Queen Mary passed through an epoch? She achieved for herself what may be called a permanent appearance which never seemed in the least old-fashioned.

Queen Victoria sustained by her own immense self-confidence was still living in 1867 when she celebrated her Diamond Jubilee 30 years later: her last days were darkened by the South African War and too late she tried to repair her neglect of Ireland that did so much to make estrangement inevitable.

Queen Mary managed to preserve the past without ever losing touch with the present, and it is well to remember in appreciating that achievement what Queen Mary had to live through without ever once indulging in self-pity let it be added.

The First World War, the Second World War, the Abdication, the loss of her husband, the loss of three sons, the loss of the India which she and King George had so much loved, the loss of Ireland which she and King George had so much hoped to keep within the United Kingdom, the agitation for women's suffrage, the strife between Lords and Commons, the General Strike . . . but the list can be protracted almost indefinitely, and to it must be added all the material progress of her time.

We cannot help being disappointed that Queen Mary did not live to see the Coronation of Queen Elizabeth II., who for those of us who can remember the Princess May of long ago recalls so much of that grandmother at the same age, and we know how much it would have gladdened Queen Mary to see that radiant occasion.

Yet somehow there is a sense of fulfilment, as if she felt so secure of the monarchy's future that her Nunc Dimittis could be said in a profound peace. And so Queen Mary has passed on: the living embodiment of two momentous centuries of monarchy is no longer with the people she served so well and who loved her so dearly.

Nevertheless, although with her an epoch ended Queen Mary has bequeathed to the new epoch a rainbow bridge with the solid past which augurs for our country a stable future.

The Lying-In-State And The Funeral

AT 2.30 this afternoon Queen Mary's coffin will leave the Queen's Chapel, beside Marlborough House, for the first stage of its journey.

It will be carried on a gun carriage in the procession that will go by way of Marlborough Gate across Horse Guards Parade, through Horse Guards Arch, and down Whitehall to Westminster Hall. Service men will line the route.

The bearer party—members of the Queen's Company of Grena… Guards—and the pall-…rs—colonels of Queen …'s regiments—will walk …side the gun carriage. …hind it will walk the four … Dukes—the Duke of Edin-…h, the Duke of Gloucester, … Duke of Windsor, and the …e of Kent. Then will come …nbers of the foreign royal …ilies followed by the other …e members of the British …yal Family. (The Queen and …er women members of the family will go to Westminster Hall by car.)

Next will come members of Queen Mary's personal household, detachments of Queen Mary's regiments and Nursing Services, followed by diplomats, British officials from abroad, and others. Finally will come a company of the Brigade of Guards.

This procession, which is due at Westminster Hall at 2.55 p.m., will be described in a B.B.C. programme on both the Home and Light wavelengths at 2.20 and televised from 2.30

Once at Westminster Hall, the coffin will be placed on the catafalque. A short service will be conducted there by the Archbishop of Canterbury. Mr. Churchill, members of the Cabinet, Mr. Attlee, peers, and M.P.s are expected to be present at this ceremony, which will be broadcast on the Home and Light wavelengths, and as a sound only programme on television.

At 4 p.m. Westminster Hall will be opened to the public for the lying-in-state. It will remain open until 3 a.m. on Tuesday (except for two hours—from 6 a.m. until 8 a.m.—tomorrow).

The scene at Westminster Hall will be televised at 8 o'clock tonight, and a description of it by Richard Dimbleby will be broadcast at 9.15, followed by a feature programme on Queen Mary in which her friends will pay personal tributes to her memory.

Then, early on Tuesday morning, the coffin will be taken to the Albert Memorial Chapel at Windsor Castle, privately.

The funeral service itself will be held in St. George's Chapel, Windsor, at 11 a.m.

The B.B.C. will broadcast the service from 10.50 a.m. until 11.45 a.m. on both Light and Home wavelengths.

That is a by-invitation-only service, but a public memorial service will be held at St. Paul's Cathedral at 3 p.m. on Tuesday. There is room for 3,500 people in St. Paul's, but 1,500 of them will have to stand.

LOST DIPLOMATS 'IN BERLIN'

THE missing British Foreign Office men, Burgess and McLean, appeared in the U.S. sector of Berlin six months after they disappeared, according to Soviet Zone deputy premier, Otto Nuschke in Bonn, yesterday.

He added: "My government has written proof of it."

But he dragged in Burgess and McLean in trying to get out of answering reporters' questions about the West Berlin anti-Communist lawyer, Walter Linse, who was kidnapped in the U.S. sector by Red agents three months ago.

WEST EUROPE AND EMPIRE LINK PLANNED

A PLAN to make Europe independent of dollar aid by forming an economic union between the British Commonwealth and Western Europe's overseas territories has been approved by the Council of Europe's Economic Sub-committee in Strasbourg.

Mr. Robert Boothby, M.P., British delegate to the Council's Consultative Assembly, said that under the plan, the system of Commonwealth preference would be widened to allow secondary preferences to be extended—to French North Africa for example.

Everest men honoured

ETH: (*appears in door, smiling*) Want to see something that'll do your heart good, Mr Glum. Look!

She makes way. Ron, shy and a bit embarrassed, appears dressed in his new clothes. Mr Glum is quite moved.

MR GLUM: Oh, Ron! You may not ever wind up a captain of industry, but, looking like that, I tell you this — you're bound to make lance-corporal.

RON: I feel a bit silly, Dad.

MR GLUM: Silly? Didn't you *listen* to Eth? Smartness is never silly.

RON: I didn't mean that, Dad. I meant coming home here then having to go all the way back again.

ETH: Back a —? You mean your interview's at a shop in the Parade?

RON: (*nods — looks at green card he's holding*) Number twenty-three.

MR GLUM: (*a qualm*) Did you say twenty-three?

RON: (*peering at card*) Some kind of gents' outfitters.

MR GLUM: (*heart sinking*) What'll you bet, Eth? What'll you bet? (*Snatches card, looks at it*) Messrs Loveday Brothers!

As he snatches off Ron's trilby and belabours him with it, playout music and
BLACKOUT.

THE BATH

GERMS MEET WASTE-PIPE WATERLOO!

For your home — JEYPINE'S Pleasant

Out of doors always use **JEYES' FLUID** to maintain freshness and cleanliness. Goes twice as far and is the most economical. Sizes and

Bronco The DE LUXE TOILET PAPER

GUARANTEED 100% PURE and ASEPTO

I always use SANIZAL to keep germs and smells away — it's stronger and cheaper

SAN IZAL DISINFECTANT

THE HOME DISINFECTANT

LIFEBUOY TOILET SOAP protects you longer —really stops B.O. (body odour)

You'll feel sure and confident after a bath with Lifebuoy Toilet Soap because its protection lasts and lasts. The fragrant freshness given by Lifebuoy Toilet Soap will delight you.

Lifebuoy Toilet Soap's new, purifying ingredient brings you lasting freshness — its invigorating lather gets rid of stale perspiration (B.O.) where it starts. And millions of discriminating Lifebuoy Toilet Soap users love its new perfume, too — they find its fragrance so exhilarating. Try the big new Bath Size tonight.

The Pub, night. Pub hubbub, over which:

LANDLORD: (*shouting*) Time, gentlemen, please! All your glasses please, gents. Come on, Mr Glum, please let me get finished up early tonight. It's my bath-night, Mr Glum, and you know how much I love a good old soak.

MR GLUM: Yes, I've met her. But don't you talk to me about bath-nights, Ted. Not after what happened to *me* last week. Cor! That was something I shall remember till the day I die — if I'm spared that long. What happened was — (*Changing to gently chiding tone*) — Ah, Ted, you weren't about to pour yet *another* brown ale in this glass, were you?

LANDLORD: No I wasn't, Mr Glum.

MR GLUM: (*grimly*) I thought you weren't! So shove one in there. No, reverting to last week, what happened was, I'd gone up to have a bath at my usual time — first of the month — and downstairs I'd left my son Ron — you know my boy Ron, don't you?

LANDLORD: He the one with the Tommy Steele haircut?

MR GLUM: That's him. Except it's not a Tommy Steele haircut, it's a Davy Crockett hat gone mangy. Anyway, while I'm upstairs, he's on the sofa in our front room with his fiancée, Eth. And what *transpired* — as it transpires ...

Music, and we hark back to the Glums' sitting-room, night.

Ron and Eth are on the sofa.

ETH: Oh Ron ... Your father started having his bath at seven — it's now gone ten and he's still up there! That can't be good for an old man. Why should he be in that bath for three hours?

RON: Perhaps he's a *dirty* old man.

ETH: Even so, no one should stay in there all that time. I mean, I like my bath, but even allowing for a good old wallow — I'm in and out in twenty minutes. Oh, wouldn't you like to just pop your head round the bathroom door?

RON: (*eagerly*) Oh yes, Eth.

ETH: Your *father's* door! Please, Ron, please pop up and make sure nothing's happened to him.

RON: I'd rather not, Eth. I already popped up once — just after he got into the bath. He threw the dirty linen at me.

ETH: Why-ever for?

RON: (*resentful*) Just 'cos I put Lady Barnett in there with him.

ETH: Lady Barnett?

RON: My goldfish. Poor little thing's got to stretch her fins somewhere.

ETH: But that's even more worrying, Ron. If Mr Glum got into one of his *rages* ... ! A heavily-built man like him all worked-up in a steamy little bathroom ... ! Ron, he could go out just like *that*!

RON: Oh no, he couldn't go out like that, Eth. He'd be arrested.

ETH: What I meant, Ron—

RON: (*firmly*) Look, Eth, you're just making a mountain out of a mole-hole. Dad's all right. If anything had happened to him, we'd have heard.

From upstairs comes a muffled shout of infuriated frustration ...

ETH: Ron, isn't that him? Listen.

From upstairs, more unintelligible shouting. This time, a muffled tirade of baffled profanity.

RON: (*triumphant*) There, Eth. See? (*Fondly*) He's singing!

ETH: That was no singing, Ron. He's in difficulties! (*Shout*) Mr Glum, are you feeling all right?

The bathroom. Mr Glum is in the bath.

MR GLUM: (*furious shout*) All right? No, I'm not all right. I can't get meself out of the *bath*!

The sitting-room.

ETH: (*getting up*) I knew it, Ron. I had a premonition. (*Calls*) How ill *are* you, Mr Glum?

The bathroom.

MR GLUM: (*shout*) Who's talking about *ill*? Me big toe's stuck in the perishing plug-hole!

As he tugs his leg, music and we go back to the pub, night.

LANDLORD: Well, strike me rotten! Got your big toe jammed in the plug-hole? Dear oh dear. Must have been a bit unpleasant, I should think.

MR GLUM: (*heavy sarcasm*) Oh no, Ted, it was delightful. If there's one thing I can thoroughly recommend, it's sitting for three hours in rapidly cooling water, with your toe stuck in the waste-pipe, and a flipping goldfish sporting round your southern hemisphere.

LANDLORD: Still you were lucky your Ron and Eth were there to lend a hand. Come to think of it, though, Eth couldn't have been that much help, really. Not in the circumstances.

MR GLUM: Well, as it happens, we got *round* that particular difficulty. I told Ron to empty a few packets of gravy-browning into the bath water.

LANDLORD: Gravy browning ... ? Oh, that was shrewd, Mr Glum. That really was shrewd.

MR GLUM: Shrewd enough for *you* to think about pouring some brown in? (*Offers glass. As landlord pours —*) Yes, it worked a treat. By the time Ron had emptied the twelfth packet in, I'd have got a 'U' Certificate from any Watch Committee in the country. 'Course he had to stir it *round* a little ...

Music and we're back in the bathroom, night.

The bath is the old-fashioned kind, with no front panel enclosing it. Mr Glum's bath-water is now deep brown and Ron is stirring it with a wooden toy-spade.

MR GLUM: That's it, Ron, give it a good swish round. Want to try one more packet for luck?

Ron pours in packet of brand-name gravy-browning. There's a knock on door.

Outside the bathroom door. Eth is knocking.

ETH: All right for me to come in yet, Mr Glum?

MR GLUM: (*from inside*) Hang on, Eth! How's it seem to *you*, Ron?

RON: (*from inside*) Just a minute, Dad.

The bathroom. Ron is licking his lips.

RON: Lovely.

MR GLUM: I didn't mean *taste* it! (*Peering*) Oh, it seems dark enough now. (*Calls*) Right ho, Eth, I'm decent.

The door opens and Eth enters.

ETH: Hallo, Mr Glum.

MR GLUM: (*weak voice*) Hallo, my dear. You'll pardon me not getting up. Well, Eth, this is a fine predicament for a man of my years to find himself in, eh? Sitting here like The Browning Version.

ETH: It's too awful, Mr Glum. But what did you want to put your big toe in the plug-hole for in the first place?

MR GLUM: (*irritable*) I didn't *want* to put it in. I had to put it in! There wasn't no plug.

ETH: No plug?

MR GLUM: This afternoon, my son — your husband-to-be — he went round and collected the plug from the bath, the plug from the basin, the plug from the kitchen sink, both knobs off the telly and the check lino out the scullery.

ETH: Ron — whatever for?

RON: I'm teaching myself draughts.

MR GLUM: Consequence was, when I turned on the tap this evening — what happened? The water runs straight out.

ETH: Tt! Yes, it would, wouldn't it?

MR GLUM: Never mind it would, wouldn't it, it did, didn't it? The only thing I could do was get undressed, place myself in the *empty* bath and this time, prior to turning the taps on, stuff me big toe down the plug-hole. That part alone gave me a severe emotional shock.

ETH: Emotional shock?

MR GLUM: You try sitting down naked on cold porcelain! But at least the bath filled up all right, so — after passing a lightly-soaped flannel over my salient features, I lay me head back in the water, did my walrus impersonation — then went to get *out*. And what did I find? That toe was stuck fast! Wedged like a bung in a beer-barrel! Nothing'll shift it!

ETH: And that's how you've been for three hours? Oh, Ron, he hasn't even had any supper. Shouldn't you bring him up some?

RON: I think that might make him feel worse, Eth.

ETH: Why, Ron?

RON: It was toad in the hole.

MR GLUM: Cor lummy, it's like Fate itself is perspiring against me.

ETH: Now, try not to get embittered, Mr Glum. (*Gazing at hidden toe*) There must be *some* way of — look, how about this. Suppose we put a broomstick under your knee, wedge it against the side of the bath, then Ron and I throw all our weight on the other end. What would happen?

ght Night"—last Monday—and Harringay's—Tue olling again. The big shows will be with us fro ain. And certainly during that.

LEAGUE CLUB CAPTAINS
No. 19
JOE MERCER of ARSENAL

POPULAR Joe Mercer of Arsenal started his climb up the soccer ladder of fame when he joined the Goodison Park ground staff as a 15-year-old inside-right in the mid-thirties. Last season he reached the top rung, when, within the space of twenty-four April hours, he received "The Footballer Of The Year" trophy and the F.A. Cup.

The Cup-winners' medal awarded to him as captain of the victorious Arsenal side completed the Mercer collection of football honours. He thus captained England; Arsenal when they won the 1947-48 League Championship and in their year of Cup triumph.

Everton scouts first spotted Joe shining in Merseyside junior circles, and, after graduating through the Central League ranks of the "Toffee's," he made his League bow at inside right against Leeds United.

His conversion to wing-half soon followed, and he enjoyed his finest season in 1938-39 when he made 41 League appearances for the Everton side that carried off the First Division title and was "capped" five times for England.

Joe played 28 times for wartime England, when the national half-line of Britton-Cullis-Mercer won soccer immortality. In addition, he played in all three Victory internationals of 1945-46.

Mercer was again among the headlines in November 1946, when he joined a relegation-fighting Arsenal at a fee of £7,000. Since then he has made 157 League appearances for the Highbury club.

Interesting fact concerning goal-maker Joe is that his next goal for Arsenal will be his first in either League or Cup. His only goal for the "Gunners" was against the Racing Club de Paris in 1949.

ne end
mpress
Danny
him-
Jim
ll be
Con-
rles

he
ld
wn!
n!.

FISH, Harlow middleweight unbeaten run. One of the thers who are rapidly national fame, Bobby is aged by Jack Carey.

seat. I have on many ailed the fact that cer-
adopt the "sergeant-
e towards boxers. But
y I have watched with interest
one or whose interference with fighters'
cause me to work has caused me to christen him
"The Natterer."

MR GLUM: You'd break my ruddy *leg*, that's what would happen! Do you think I haven't been cudgelling my brains for a way out. There isn't one. I tell you, Ethel, I won't be shifted from this bathroom without major surgery! All because my dear son took it into his head to — (*Emits a sudden, surprisingly maidenly shriek*)

ETH: What is it?

MR GLUM: That rotten *goldfish*! Keeps doing that when I least *expect* it. Where is it? (*Grabbing about in the dark water*) Just let me get my hands on it. I'll teach it to treat me likè a subterranean grotto! (*Paddles his hand round*)

RON: Watch it, Dad. You thrash around like that, you'll thin your gravy.

MR GLUM: It's all so inexplainable. If the perishing toe went in, why won't it come out?

ETH: Oh, that's quite easily explainable, Mr Glum. It was the heat of the hot water.

MR GLUM: Eh?

ETH: It made your big toe swell. You see, heat always makes things get bigger.

RON: She's quite right, Dad. That's why days are longer in the summer than they are in the winter.

MR GLUM: Thank you very much. So your suggestion is that I sit here till the winter?

ETH: Oh no, Mr Glum, But we're on the right track.

MR GLUM: How d'you mean?

ETH: Well, if we could — Ron, can you think of some way for your father to cool his big toe down?

RON: I think so, Eth.

MR GLUM: How, Ron?

RON: Well, it seems obvious to me, Dad.

MR GLUM: All right, don't keep it a secret. How can I cool that toe down?

RON: Take it out and blow on it.

MR GLUM: (*containing his feelings*) Take it out and ... Ron?

RON: Yes, Dad?

MR GLUM: Once and for all, *admit* something to me. I just want the satisfaction of hearing you admit it.

RON: What, Dad?

MR GLUM: Sometimes you're as dim as a sweep's ear-'ole! Aren't you?

RON: Yes, Dad.

MR GLUM: Not just 'Yes, Dad'. Admit it.

RON: Sometimes I'm as dim as a sweep's ear-'ole.

MR GLUM: Just plain honest-to-goodness gormless.

RON: Just plain honest-to-goodness gormless.

MR GLUM: And stupid *with* it.

RON: And stupid *with* it.

MR GLUM: Thank you, Ron. At least, that's made me feel a *little* better.

RON: I tell you one thing about me though, Dad.

MR GLUM: What's that?

RON: I've never got my big toe stuck in a plug-hole.

MR GLUM: (*to Eth, wildly*) Either take him away or — ! (*Inspecting his hand*) Look at me flesh — it's started going all *crinkly*. What with that and the gravy, I'll be like the edge of a steak-and-kidney pie. Please, Eth — think!

ETH: We are thinking, Mr Glum. You really musn't be so impatient.

MR GLUM: Impatient? For heaven's sake, what am I asking? If they can raise ninety thousand tons of shipping out the Suez Canal, surely you two can get one old man's toe out a waste-pipe.

ETH: Waste-pipe! Yes, of course — that is a *pipe*, isn't it! I'd forgotten that. Ron — why don't we tackle the problem the other way about?

RON: You mean push his *head* in?

ETH: No, Ron. Get at the toe from the other end of the waste-pipe!

MR GLUM: Ah! Now that's the first sensible suggestion yet. Yes — 'stead of *pulling* at the toe, get to a position where you can *push* at it from beneath. Ron —

RON: Yes, Dad?

MR GLUM: Bend down and have a look at the bottom of the bath.

RON: Right ho, Dad.

Ron sticks his head straight down into the bath-water.

MR GLUM: (*gazing fascinated*) Trouble is, you see, Eth — his mind has never really caught up with his body.

ETH: Mr Glum, he'll drown!

Ron's head comes out of the water, gasping and spluttering.

RON: (*breathing hard*) Couldn't see *anything*, Dad. There was a toe in the way.

MR GLUM: And the moment I get back the use of that toe, I know exactly where I'm going to place it. (*Patiently*) Ron, look *underneath* the bath. (*Points*) Down under the plug-hole. What you should find there is a waste-pipe coming out and forming a 'U'.

RON: A 'U'.

MR GLUM: A 'U'. And at the base of that 'U' there is a nut.

RON: A nut.

MR GLUM: A nut. Or, if you prefer — 'U' again. Now if you go and *undo* that nut, you will perceive a *hole* which, if you shove something up it, you can easily reach my ill-fated toe. Do you understand?

MR GLUM AND RON: (*pause; then, together*) No, Dad.

During that exchange, Eth has gone to the tap-end and is now crouching there, with a hand underneath.

ETH: I've got it, Ron. And it unscrews quite ... (*grunt*) ... Ah! (*Exhibits a nut — bends and peers underneath*) And there's the hole — oh, it can only be a couple of inches from the end of Mr Glum's toe. (*Getting up*) Quick, Ron, get something out the bathroom cabinet you can shove up and push with.

RON: (*reaching inside cabinet*) Right ho, Eth.

As Eth comes to Mr Glum's head, Ron goes off to tap-end.

ETH: This'll do it, Mr Glum. You're only a few seconds away from freedom now. See where you've got to push up, Ron?

RON: (*crouching*) I see, Eth. Ready, Dad?

MR GLUM: I been ready for three hours. A good hard push now, son.

RON: Right ho, Dad. (*Grunt of effort*)

MR GLUM: (*howl of agony*) Aagh! What did you —?

RON: (*exhibiting scissors*) You said find something to —

MR GLUM: You great brainless —! That hole's only a couple of *inches* from where my toe is. You should be able to push it out with your finger.

RON: My finger. Ah! (*Holds up left hand, inspects it*) Question is ... No, I've got a taller one somewhere. (*Brings up right hand, extends forefinger*) Ah, thought so. Stand by, Dad. (*Drops to crouch, reaches right hand under bath*)

MR GLUM: Feel me toe?

RON: Just a mo', just a mo' ... Ah! Contact!

MR GLUM: (*excited*) Now *push*, lad. *Hard*! All your weight behind it. I can feel it moving, moving — one more ought to ... (*Triumph*) Aah! (*His foot pops out of water*)

ETH: Oh, the poor thing. Look —

Mr Glum's toe has a well-defined red ring round it.

MR GLUM: I'm free! Free! Oh, the relief, the — Eth, I can't thank you enough for — (*His voice breaks*)

ETH: Oh, that's all right.

MR GLUM: And Ron — them remarks I made about you being dim and gormless and stupid ... well, I apologize, son. It was just the heat of the moment. Will you — will you shake hands and say you forgive your nasty-tempered old Daddy?

RON: (*eyes cast down*) No, I won't, Dad.

MR GLUM: Oh no, Ron, don't bear grudges. Come on, sonny boy, shake hands.

RON: I just can't, Dad.

MR GLUM: What do you mean 'can't'?

RON: It's my finger. (*Tugging*) I can't seem to —

MR GLUM: Oh, gawd no! Oh, you dim, gormless, stupid, no-good —

As Eth runs to Ron and vainly tries hauling at his arm, playout music and BLACKOUT.

Christmas Shopping by Post See Page 2

DAILY HERALD

No. 12677 (C)   WEATHER: Cold. Some rain—See Page 3.   RADIO and TV—See Page 4.   PRICE 2D

SATURDAY LONDON SPECIAL   DEC 1 1956

Tax cut by half on pianos

IT will be cheaper to buy a handbag for a Christmas present this year. And a piano will cost only half as much tax. From today on—

POISON RIDDLE OF HAPPY WIFE

By Robert Traini

GINGER BURDETT and his attractive young wife were drinking tea at breakfast in their little two-room flat. They smiled at the chattering of their three-year-old son lying in bed in the next room.

Suddenly Mrs. Burdett clutched her heart and collapsed. By the time an ambulance had got her to hospital she was dead.

From a heart attack, it was thought.

But yesterday a post-mortem examination revealed that the cause of death was cyanide poisoning.

Last night Det.-Supt. Albert Webb and Det.-Insp. Harry Cox were trying to discover who poisoned her. Had she a secret enemy?

For neighbours of red-haired, 24-year-old Brian and 21-year-old Moira Burdett say they seemed happy, though she "kept herself to herself" and rarely went out.

Vegetables

Mrs. Burdett died on Wednesday, and the day before she went to the greengrocer's opposite her home in Appleford-road, North Kensington, and bought potatoes and carrots.

The manager of the shop said: "After she died Mr. Burdett came over and asked what had had bought."

She had also bought some rolls and milk.

Detectives do not yet know how the cyanide was taken, nor how much.

They have failed also to discover if Mrs. Burdett ever produced any cyanide.

Neighbours have been asked if a stranger had been seen entering the flat recently.

Last night Mr. Burdett and his child Raymond were staying with the father's family in West London.

America is sure we are quitting Egypt so—

IKE ROLLS OUT THE BARRELS

WASHINGTON, Friday.—Confident that Britain and France really mean to get out of Egypt, President Eisenhower tonight started rushing emergency oil to Western Europe.

A U.S. super-tanker carrying 30,000 tons has been ordered to take its cargo to Britain instead of Philadelphia.

Forty more tankers are being taken out of "mothballs" to help in the great oil lift.

The President has ordered anti-trust laws to be waived so that 15 big oil companies can co-ordinate their efforts.

Still short, unless...

A tremendous stepping up of production is planned in the Venezuelan and U.S. Gulf Coast oilfields, where output is normally restricted.

But Washington officials warned that whatever America may be able to do, there will still be a shortage of about 20 per cent. in Western Europe while the Suez Canal remains closed and the Middle East pipelines cut.

Usually reliable sources said that America could provide up to 1,100,000 barrels a day from the Western Hemisphere.

An announcement by the Office for Defence Mobilisation said: "The present problem is transportation—the number of tankers available is not sufficient to maintain oil consumption at normal levels everywhere in the world.

"The co-ordination of industry efforts will insure the most efficient use of tankers and the maximum availability of petroleum products."

Signal at sea

What we say

OUT!

We are getting out of Egypt. However the Government may also be out. A hundred Tory back-bench Samsons are threatening to pull it down.

This would be a benefit to our unfortunate country. For the Government, having thrust us into a disastrous failure in Egypt, is now plunging us into economic calamity with which it is incompetent to deal.

It was getting into difficulties before the Egyptian crisis. It has not shot its way out of any difficulties. It has shot the nation into a hideous new mess.

Unless there is a rapid change, this country may be down as well as out.

TURKEY CALLS UP TROOPS AS ARAB FEARS MOUNT

TURKEY, alarmed by reports of massive Russian military aid to Syria, last night recalled certain army reservists to the colours.

They are to take part in what are called "routine manoeuvres."

A communiqué issued in Istanbul said the call-up and the manoeuvres are "normal measures." But, the communiqué added, it is natural for the Turkish armed forces to take vigilant measures in accordance with the present circumstances.

The Turks have not yet answered accusations by Russia and Syria that Turkey and Iraq are planning a military attack on Syria.

But the accusations were enough to alert Turkey's defences. She shares a 500-mile frontier with Syria and has common frontier with Russia stretches for 200 miles.

In London, Mr. Menderes, the Turkish Foreign Minister, had a long talk with Mr. Selwyn Lloyd.

The main theme of their talk was Turkey's growing anxiety about the Russian arming of Syria and Turkey's desire for a strengthening of the Bagdad Pact.

Martial law in Iraq

PEOPLE were killed in clashes between police and demonstrators in Northern Iraq, according to Cairo Radio. Martial law has been declared.

Bagdad Radio said the military commander of Northern Iraq, General Saadi Ali, had warned against "subversive and Communist instigations."

The General declared that trouble-makers were trying to get people to strike and close their shops.

"Such activities," he said, "must stop. Strict measures will be taken against those who violate my orders."

Syria talks of threats

SYRIA'S delegate to the United Nations, Dr. Zeineddine, told a Press conference in New York last night of an Anglo-French build-up on Syria's border.

He claimed that France had stationed half a division and 100 planes in Israel.

He alleged, too, that British officers and technicians were in Israel ready for an act of

My mother —by Lord Hailsham

LORD HAILSHAM, First Lord of the Admiralty, addressed some remarkable words to America last night. And four times he pointed out that his mother was an American.

He said at once that he would find it easier to speak—he was talking to Oxford Conservatives—"not as a Minister, but simply "as the son of an American mother."

He said: "I cannot turn against America about turning against my own mother, and that I cannot do.

"But for the first time since the war, almost for the first time in my life, I find it hard to say I am half American and still harder to say that I am proud of it."

Lord Hailsham said that while the Tories — didn't mind being criticised.

"But we will not be insulted. We don't want hear any moral lectures.

'MY DUTY'

Lord Hailsham had hard words for Pres. Eisenhower.

"It is my duty, as if of an American mother said, to tell him that allows Europe to go short of oil this winter and to build up a pond of misery and unemployment, it will be no good then to say that our friendship stands.

"America will have no friends west of Suez if her Government allows that."

Lord Hailsham complained bitterly that America had frustrated the British Navy's efforts to clear the Canal.

IN PARIS yesterday accepted a Russian offer to increase oil supplies to France from 350,000 tons a year to 650,000 tons in 1957, rising to 1,906,000 in 1958.

PINEAU MEETS LLOYD—BUT IT'S HUSH-HUSH

THE French Foreign Minister spent most of yesterday discussing the Egyptian situation with Mr. Selwyn Lloyd. After they had dined together M. Pineau flew back

Police hunt for missing couple

POLICE stepped up their hunt last night for a woman of 57 and her 34-year-old second husband who have vanished since they went on a car trip five days ago.

A note was left by the woman, Mrs. Mary Love, mother of six children by her first marriage, at the couple's home in Portland-road, Tottenham, at 12.45 p.m. on Monday. It said, "Be back at 1.30 p.m."

She and her husband, John (*pictured above on their wedding day a year ago*) left home in a black Wolseley saloon, registration DPE 343.

Mr. Love, an ex-Merchant Navy officer, had a medical appointment at the RAF Employment Bureau, Euston, at 1.30 p.m. He did not turn up.

Nor is there any trace of the car which had petrol only for about 40 miles.

Last night, in the family's lounge, Mrs. Love's blonde daughter Maureen, who is 19, told me how she introduced the couple before their marriage.

She said: "I was going out with my stepfather's brother James. One night James brought John to the house we then had at Barnet.

"He became a lodger. When we moved to Tottenham, he moved with my mother and the rest of the family."

Mr. Love, who had an RAF disability pension, had been "under the care of a doctor."

DAUGHTER MAUREEN *She introduced them.*

Car city is warned 'Fewer jobs soon'

WITHIN the next two weeks petrol rationing may put nearly 20,000 car workers on short time in Coventry *alone*. Many others may face sackings. This was the crisis warning given yesterday ... Coventry District ...king and ...

DETECTIVES CHECK ON BABY'S DEATH

The death of an 11-month-old baby in married quarters at Newton RAF station, Nottinghamshire, is being investigated by the county CID.

An inquest on the child, Stuart Thomas Smith, son of a RAF corporal, was adjourned yesterday for a fortnight. The baby died from asphyxia, accelerated by asphyxia, the coroner was told.

CHAPLIN SHOCK U.S. BID TO KEEP HIM OUT

Tory says Suez get-out will bring down the Cabinet

THE Conservative Party is in danger of being split allow the Government of my country to throw it away.

hold the country and the Conservative Party together only by standing firm and requiring the

THE TORTOISE

Malenkov tells Britain:
U.S. bases are a peril

EORGI MALENKOV, Russian
Deputy Premier and the man
ped as Stalin's successor, told
itain yesterday that leasing cf air
ses to the United States had placed
r in a dangerous position.

Malenkov devoted most of his speech
the Russian Communist Party congress
a bitter attack on the United States,
lling Americans warmongers and empire
rabbers.

Britain, he said, was carrying out a policy
ctated by the U.S.
already brought great suffering

Acheson—we are undivided

CHURCHILL ASKS TITO, 'COME TO BRITAIN'

MARSHAL TITO handing Foreign Minister Anthony Eden a
cigarette during a reception in Belgrade. In the centre is the
Marshal's wife Jovanka making her first public appearance since
the announcement of her marriage.

KENYA: a dangerous situation

From Arthur Webb

FROM the British colony of
Kenya, in East Africa, comes
a rush of stories about the
rrible Mau Mau. Weird stories,

Ike hit by 'millionaire' scandal

WASHINGTON, Friday.
GENERAL EISENHOWER ran
up against new embarrass-
ments from his Republican
friends today. His vice-presidential candidate, Senator
Nixon, was accused of being
subsidised by millionai—
Disclos—

are worried. They fear they may
have to abandon their charges
against the Democrats which have
ne of their best weapons.
of Ike's staff are already
him to ask for Nixon's
on as vice-presidential
e.

them blurted out in the
op tour train
It's just m
self is con
nd Earl
didates for

nomination. He showed his
embarrassment when he sent a
message to the reporters later
that he intended to phone Nixon
about the allegation of "non-
ethical practices."

He added, however: "I believe
Dick Nixon to be an honest man.
I am confident he will place the
facts before the American people
fairly and squarely."

Senator Nixon himself is trying
to gloss over the whole
which accuse

Churchill, Eden and Butler now away

The Government's
Ministers will
country will

Supremo needed for cold war

UPREME Allied commander should
e appointed to wage and win the
war for the free world, Field-Marshal
unt Montgomery declared last night.
was because we lost cold wars that
ad to fight hot ones, he said.
e tackle a potentially hot war on
llied basis. Why do we not do the
for the cold war?" he asked.
e enslaved peoples had to be shown
life on our side of the Iron Curtain
better than what was going on on
side.

To win the cold war two things were
essential: (1) An agreed Allied plan;
(2) Effective machinery for handling the
problem.

Of the future, he said: "Our aim
remains unchanged—it is peace. Our
motto should be: No infirmity of purpose."

Lord Montgomery, Deputy Supreme
Commander in Europe, was speaking at
Chatham House, London, to mark the
publication to-day of "Atlantic Alliance,"

a report by a study group of the Royal
Institute of International Affairs.

The report urges closer consultation
and planning in foreign policy for
Europe and towards Russia.

The study group "see no reason to
revise the view that the Soviet Government and their Chinese ally wish for the
time being to avoid world war, but recog-
nise that the risks of miscalculation and
misinformation in the Kremlin may be
greater than was once thought."

COME BACK OR RESIGN

SIR ANTHONY EDEN
should return from Ja-
maica or resign, declared Mr.
Harold Wilson, M.P. last
night.

He was speaking to the Oxford
University Labour Club.

Mr. Wilson said: "Everyone
sympathises with the Prime
Minister in his illness. The
country would have understood

it if he had gone away for a
complete rest, leaving a Deputy
Premier in charge with full
authority to act.

"But there is no Deputy
Prime Minister. There is no
official acting Prime Minister.
Y e hear that at this
time the Prime Minister, 4,860
miles by air from London, is
having trunk telephone lines
fixed in his bungalow and is

Harold Wilson tells Eden

turning his rest home into an
office.

"Who is in charge? Either
the Prime Minister is too ill to
be entrusted with the government of the country, or if he is
fit enough to interfere, he is fit
enough to return home

"What this country has the
right to say to Sir Anthony Eden
at this time is: Return—or resign."

The pub, evening. Pub hubbub – over which:

LANDLORD: (*shouting*) Time, gentlemen, please. Drink up, please, Mr Glum. Here, Mr Glum – didn't I see you in the pet shop one day during the week?

MR GLUM: Yes, Ted, you did. I took my boy Ron along to see the man there.

LANDLORD: (*sympathetic*) Oh, dear.

MR GLUM: Not 'cos of Ron being out-of-sorts! To buy him a pet. We used to have this little budgerigar, you see, but Monday afternoon, it – well, it disappeared.

LANDLORD: Disappeared?

MR GLUM: Can't understand it. It was definitely there Monday morning when I cleaned out its cage with the vacuum cleaner. But Ron was so upset I sent him off to get another pet. A bigger one this time, some animal that could be more of a pal to him. Well, Ted, you should have seen him that evening . . .

Music – and we hark back to the Glums' sitting-room, evening.

Ron and Eth are on the sofa, watching a tortoise on the carpet in front of them.

ETH: Oh, Ron . . . you'll never make him sit up and beg if you frighten him. Give him here.

RON: No, Eth. He's my tortoise! I'll make him do it yet. (*Picking up a chair and holding it before him with its legs extended, like a lion tamer, he advances on tortoise*) Come on now, boy – beg! Up! *Up, sir* . . ! Oh, Eth, he's pulled his head in again.

ETH: I should think so. That's no way to train a tortoise. Now just put that chair down. First thing you've got to do, beloved, is make the little chap answer to his name.

RON: But I don't know his name.

ETH: Well, give him one. Now is it a boy or a girl?

RON: (*patiently*) It's a tortoise, Eth.

ETH: Well, of course, Ron. But even an animal has to be one or the other. So can you think of a name which is both male *and* female?

RON: (*thinks; then*) . . . 'Mixed Bathing'?

ETH: Ye-e-es . . . But I meant more of a namey name. One that could be either for a boy or a girl. Like, well – 'Dopey'.

RON: Oh no, Eth. I've only ever heard that applied to a masculine.

ETH: Are you sure, Ron?

RON: 'Course I'm sure, Eth – I'm not deaf. I'll tell you one – 'Laurence Olivia'.

ETH: 'Laurence Olivia'?

RON: Well, that could be both. Laurence is a boy's name and Olivia is a girl's name.

ETH: Ron, that's very shrewd. Go on then, try it on him. Or her. See if he answers. Or her.

RON: Right. *(He calls softly)* Laurence Olivia! Laurence Olivia . . . Laurence! Olivia! . . . (Pause) 'Mixed Bathing'! . . . *(Pause)* He hasn't stuck his head out, Eth.

ETH: No . . . Or she.

RON: Oh, Eth, do you think perhaps he can't find the hole? Or she? Oh, Eth, poor Laurence Olivia! He's all mixed up inside. *(Calls)* Laurence . . . Laurence! *(Taps shell hole)* This way out!

ETH: No, Ron, you must give him a minute or two to *ponder* over the name. Remember what it said in the leaflet from the pet shop? *(She picks up the leaflet; reads)* 'Tortoises are thoughtful, quiet, introspective creatures.'

RON: Oh.

ETH: 'However, during the mating-season, the large, older male will sometimes emit a loud repetitive bellow.'

Mr Glum enters from the hall.

MR GLUM: *(his usual bellow)* 'Allo, 'allo, 'allo. Oh, Ron! Are you still tickling the neck of that cold-blooded little nightmare?

RON: No, Dad, I'm playing with my tortoise.

MR GLUM: That's what I meant. Can you understand that boy of mine, Eth? When I think of all the really lovable little creatures what were on sale in that pet shop! Puppies . . . kittens . . . a dear little golden Hamstead . . ! And he chooses that beady-eyed reptile.

ETH: I think it's a creature one could get very fond of.

MR GLUM: Gives me the creeps! Seeing that skinny wrinkled neck come slowly poking out of the shell, then them cold, expressionless eyes staring at me suspiciously . . . ugh!! Reminds me of the War.

ETH: The War?

MR GLUM: Whenever I told Mrs Glum she could come out the air-raid shelter. I tell you, Eth, I'll never take to that beast if it's here for fifty years. Nasty stupid little creepy-crawly!

RON: It is not stupid. That tortoise is just as intelligent as I am.

MR GLUM: Well, don't spread that around, Ron, we might want to sell it one day. All right, if you want me to, I'll make an effort to get used to him. Let me try stroking his head.

RON: All right, Dad, I'll – (*Long pause*) Where's he gone?

ETH: Eh?

RON: (*gathering panic*) Eth, he's gone! Where's my tortoise gone? He's not here!

ETH: He must be here. Look round the floor.

RON: He's not! If you look on the floor you'll *see* him not there. He's gone! Dad, my tortoise has gone!!

MR GLUM: Oh, calm down. He can't have gone far. Lummy, it took him the whole of 'Panorama' to cross the fireside rug. Come on, Eth, have a good look round . . .

As they all get down on hands and knees – music – and we return to –

The pub, night-time.

LANDLORD: Oh, Mr Glum, what a shame. Did you find it?

MR GLUM: Nowhere, Ted. Ron was in a frightful state. Pitiful. Three o'clock in the morning he was still wandering round the streets waving a bit of lettuce and calling 'Laurence Olivia', 'Laurence Olivia'.

LANDLORD: Shame . . . You should have reported the loss to the authorities.

MR GLUM: We reported it to *everybody*, Ted. Everybody who might conceivably be of help. The police, the Lost Property Office, the RSPAYE. All next day we spent scouring the neighbourhood, but still no luck. By the evening we just couldn't think where to look next.

Music – and back we go to the Glums' sitting-room, evening.

The three are sitting about, despondent.

ETH: Well, I'm utterly baffled, Mr Glum. But one thing I'm convinced of. That tortoise is still somewhere in this house.

MR GLUM: (*tired*) Oh, have a heart, Eth. Nobody could have searched more thoroughly than *I* did. Four times I had Mrs Glum out of bed!

ETH: What about the cupboard under the stairs?

MR GLUM: What would it go in there for? Only things in there are the garden roller, and a sewing-machine, and a couple of box-mattresses, and my old army tin hat, and a set of Dickens, and the Holiday Fund.

ETH: Holiday Fund?

MR GLUM: That's a family name for it. It's usually called the gas-meter. No, Eth, if you ask me, it's – *(he notices Ron crawling around on all fours)* Ron! What are you doing now?

RON: I'm trying to work out where I'd go if I was a tortoise.

MR GLUM: Oh, for heaven's sake, do give over. We've –

ETH: No, just a minute, Mr Glum. Just a minute. I think Ron's hit it.

MR GLUM: I'll hit it if he doesn't change that posture.

ETH: Don't you remember that newspaper story? Oh, it was in all the papers. About that big animal that escaped from a pet shop. You read it, Ron. What kind of animal was it?

RON: A BOAC instructor.

ETH: That's it, beloved – except they pronounce it 'boa constrictor'. That's what it was, Mr Glum. And you know how they went about recovering that? They tempted it back.

MR GLUM: Tempted it? What with?

ETH: They got hold of a boa constrictor of the opposite sex! A lady constrictor. As a lure. So, why don't we use the same ruse? With a lady tortoise?

MR GLUM: Might work.

ETH: If we can get the pet shop man to bring one over, we can – Oh! Half a mo! I've thought of a bugbear.

RON: No, Eth. I think a tortoise'd be better.

ETH: A snag, Ron. You see, Mr Glum, we don't actually know whether Laurence Olivia is really a Laurence or an Olivia . . . If you get my meaning.

MR GLUM: I do, Eth. Yes, that is a ticklish point. Obviously we can't send for a tortoise of the opposite sex if we don't know what sex our tortoise is opposite to. I've always said it. It doesn't half complicate life, this sex business!

ETH: Unless . . . we ask the man to bring *two* tortoises. One of each.

MR GLUM: Ah, that's it. Then if Laurence is a Laurence he'll be tempted by the lady and if he's an Olivia he'll be lured by the gent.

ETH: You understand that idea, beloved?

RON: No, Eth.

MR GLUM: Well, what part *don't* you understand?

RON: What do we need the lady boa constrictor for?

MR GLUM: *(wearily)* What do we – *(Blazes)* To wrap round your perishing – !

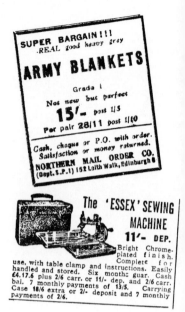

ETH: No, Mr Glum, no! Let's ring the man in the pet shop before he closes!

Music, and we come back to the Glums' sitting-room, an hour later.

Mr Glum is greeting the man from the pet shop.

MR GLUM: Very kind of you to come round so prompt, Mr Proudlock. Though I was rather hoping you'd have brought the two tortoises along with you.

MR PROUDLOCK: But I have, Mr Glum. They're under my pullover.

MR GLUM: Ah . . .I did notice but I didn't like to comment.

MR PROUDLOCK: Here we are. (*Brings forth the tortoises*) Now you'll see that on the shell of the male one I've painted a large letter 'A' – and this one marked with the letter 'B' is the female.

MR GLUM: What a good idea, Mr Proudlock. May I, in turn, introduce you to my son Ron? And this is his fiancée, Eth.

RON: The female.

MR GLUM: Now, Mr Proudlock, how do you suggest we proceed?

MR PROUDLOCK: Oh, it's quite simple. We'll put 'A' and 'B' down on the floor in front of us here and wait. If your lost tortoise is a male, he'll come out of hiding and make for tortoise 'B' – the female. If Laurence, however, is a female, she will stay where she is, and tortoise 'A' – the male – will make towards her.

ETH: (*thrilled*) Oh, isn't it romantic? How soon do you think it'll happen?

MR GLUM: Well, they got to get in the *mood* first. Ron, turn the lights down low. (*Ron does so. Mr Glum gets out a scent spray*) Now, let's spray a little of this around. It's Mrs Glum's favourite perfume. May as well use it generously, there's another quart-bottle under the sink. Now, what else? Ah . . . music! (*Tenderly la-las 'Your Eyes Are The Eyes Of A Woman In Love'*) . . . Is it having any effect?

RON: (*putting his arm round Eth*) Yes, Dad!

ETH: Ron, it's not for our benefit.

MR PROUDLOCK: Shouldn't take long. If your tortoise is a lady, we'll see 'A' moving off. If it's male, 'B' will move off.

ETH: But, Mr Proudlock, look! Look!

MR PROUDLOCK: What?

ETH: Both the tortoises are moving off! 'A' *and* 'B'!

MR GLUM: So they are! Here, Mr Proudlock, how do you account for that?

MR PROUDLOCK: (*puzzled*) I . . . I can't think . . .

RON: Perhaps it was Dad's singing.

MR GLUM: Never mind what's causing it!! They're going towards the door.

The party, headed by Ron, follow the tortoises out of the sitting-room and into the hall.

ETH: On tiptoe, everybody.

MR GLUM: And try and keep out of sight. Hey, where they gone, Ron?

RON: They've gone into the cupboard under the stairs!

MR GLUM: What they doing in there?

RON: I don't know, Dad. 'A' pushed the door closed behind him.

MR GLUM: Let's find out then. (*Opens cupboard door and pokes head in*) 'Allo, 'allo, 'allo! Well, talk about tortoise-shell spectacles! Pardon me, I'm .sure. (*Closing the door, he emerges*) Well, Mr Proudlock, so much for theory! I can assure you that neither 'A' nor 'B' are interested in any third party. He's crowding her against the sewing-machine.

RON: (*tragically*) So they won't be helping us find Laurence.

ETH: But, Mr Glum, if that's where they went, then it's probably where Laurence went as well. Oh, Mr Glum, do make sure!

MR GLUM: Oh no, Eth. I couldn't intrude again.

RON: Please, Dad. For my sake.

MR GLUM: Oh . . . all right. (*He knocks on the door, clearing his throat warningly. He opens the cupboard door and disappears inside. We hear his voice from within*) Excuse me, I won't interrupt, just want to rummage round this old junk and see if I can spot – hey! Come here, you! (*Emerges from the cupboard holding a tortoise*) Here we are, Ron. What about this?

RON: It's Laurence Olivia! (*Taking him from Mr Glum*) Dad, you found him! Oh, Laurence! (*He cradles him*)

ETH: Poor little thing. Been in there nearly twenty-four hours. But I can't understand *why!*

MR GLUM: Then let me enlighten you. While you were right on the question of the mating instinct, I was wrong on the question of intelligence. I admit now that this tortoise *has* got as much intelligence as my Ron.

ETH: What's led you to think that, Mr Glum?

MR GLUM: For the past twenty-four hours it's been trying to make love to my tin-hat!

As they gaze at Ron and the tortoise, playout music and BLACKOUT.

The pub, night-time pub hubbub – over which:

LANDLORD: *(shouting)* Time, gentlemen, please. Your last orders, gents. Drink up, if you please. Here, Mr Glum, was you trying to catch my eye earlier on?

MR GLUM: Well, not specifically your eye, Ted. I just flung that beer-rag in your *general* direction. I wanted to talk to you about your nephew. The one who's a sailor.

LANDLORD: Young George? Yes, he's about the same age as your boy Ron, isn't he? Very much brighter, of course.

MR GLUM: Now, Ted, I won't have you running down my son like that. The only thing wrong with Ron's mental capacities is that – well, he's sort of like blotting-paper.

LANDLORD: Blotting-paper?

MR GLUM: He soaks up everything – but he gets it all backwards.

LANDLORD: Then what do you want to talk to me about George for?

MR GLUM: I want to borrow him.

LANDLORD: *Borrow* George? Whatever for?

MR GLUM: Because I have a problem of father-son relationship that would baffle even that master of psychology – Signalman Freud.

LANDLORD: Get away.

MR GLUM: It come to a crux this morning. You see, yesterday my Ron did something what really angered Eth. In fact, I have never known her so put-about . . . !

Music, and we hark back to the Glums' sitting-room, daytime.

Ron and Eth are on the sofa.

ETH: Oh, Ron . . . I won't try to hide my feelings, I'm bitterly disappointed. Here's the first job you've ever been actually accepted for – and what do you do? You turn it down! *You turn it down!* I'm so blazing, I could – I could . . . *Oogh!*

RON: Well, you oogh then, Eth, if it makes you feel better.

ETH: It just brings to a head something that's been boiling up for a long time! Ron, at the risk of hurting your personal feelings, I've got to say it. You are . . . do you know what 'immature' means?

RON: When you don't get paid for doing it?

ETH: That's 'amateur'. 'Immature' means not grown-up yet! It means turning down a job because you'd have to live away from home and wouldn't be able to go running to your father with everything. *(Softening)* Oh, Ron, do you realize what you are? *Still?*

RON: Unemployed.

ETH: Besides that. You're still just a daddy's boy.

128

RON: Me?

ETH: Yes, Ron. For all your veneer of sophistication. Oh, I'm not saying you shouldn't *love* your father. But you – you look upon Mr Glum as an idol.

RON: An idol what?

ETH: You venerate him. You reckon he's the most wonderful person that ever lived, don't you?

RON: *(thinking about it)* Yes, I suppose I do, Eth. Well, him and Circus Boy.

ETH: But sometime, Ron, sometime you've got to *break away*. Strike out on your own two feet. I mean, under present circumstances – can you show me one single thing you do without getting your father to help you?

RON: *(ardently)* Yes, Eth.

ETH: No, I never meant that, Ron.

RON: Just a kiss, Eth, go on –

ETH: I couldn't be less in the mood –

The door opens and Mr Glum enters.

MR GLUM: Hallo, hallo, hallo . . . *(Sings)* 'Magic moments, bouncing on the sofa'. . . *(Chuckle)* 'Ere, Ron, give over a sec. We need to get you a fresh box of breakfast-cereal. Which sort would you like this time, son? The Marbles or the Frontier Rifle?

RON: I'll leave it to you, Dad.

ETH: *(mimicking)* 'I'll leave it to you, Dad.' Oh, Mr Glum, is your son *ever* going to think for *himself?*

MR GLUM: No call to lead off like that, Eth. Last time we had a box that gives away marbles – before I could get to him he'd already poured milk and sugar over 'em. Ooh, that *crunching* sound will haunt me . . .

ETH: And do you realize it's exactly because of that sort of coddling that he went and turned down a good paying job at Murchison Manufacturing?

MR GLUM: And quite right, too. Why should he go and cut himself off from his old Dad for something as ephemeral as mere employment? Ron's a boy who *needs* his father's care. Big as he is, he – he still comes into my bedroom of a morning for cuddles.

ETH: Cuddles!

RON: That's the name of my new tortoise, Eth. He sleeps under Dad's bed.

MR GLUM: Ron won't have him in his own room because in the middle of the night he crawls round the floor looking for bits of food. And that disturbs the tortoise.

ETH: Never *mind* the tortoise! Mr Glum, I am going to take issue with you on this and I'd rather not do it in front of Ron. So, beloved –

RON: Yes, Eth?

ETH: Would you excuse us?

RON: What have you done?

ETH: Would you leave your father and I alone for a few minutes? Is there anything you can occupy yourself with in the hall?

RON: (dubious) Well, nothing really absorbing, Eth. There's not much in the hall to – ooh, I know! I know what I can do!

ETH: What?

RON: I'll lean up against the wall.

MR GLUM: You do that, son. I'll call you when to come back.

Ron leaves the room.

MR GLUM: Now what *is* all this, Eth? I sense an undercurrent. I know you're upset about Ron turning down that job at Murchison Manufacturing but – well, I'm personally glad. Can you imagine how lonely I'd have been here without him? Bin horrible. I'd probably have ended up talking to Mrs Glum.

ETH: That's all very well from your point of view. But, sometime, Mr Glum, you've got to cut Ron loose.

MR GLUM: Eh?

ETH: While he stays with you, he's – he's just sapped of all initiative. And after all – well, you're not going to be here forever, are you?

MR GLUM: Well, 'course not. They're open in twenty-seven and three-quarter minutes –

ETH: What I'm getting at is – you've got to force Ron to leave you, Mr Glum. The only way he'll ever take that job at Murchison's is by leaving you.

MR GLUM: Leaving me? Eth, you – you don't know what you're asking. My baby boy? All right, he may be a bit over-fond of me, but – does that have to mean he can't sort out anything at all off his own initiative?

Ron comes back from the hall.

RON: Dad –

MR GLUM: What is it, Ron?

RON: I need your advice.

MR GLUM: Yes?

RON: Which wall shall I stand against?

ETH: (grimly) . . . Well, Mr Glum?

As Mr Glum shrugs miserably, music, and we return to the pub, daytime.

Lend Me Your Body for 7 Days...

and I'll Give You PROOF I Can Make YOU a NEW MAN!

— *Charles Atlas*

Charles Atlas *Winner of the title "The World's Most Perfectly Developed Man"*

No Other Physical Instructor in the World Has Ever Dared Make Such An Offer!

ALL I want is a chance to give you PROOF—in just 7 days, and right in your own home—that I can give YOU the might muscles and boundless energy you want! Right in the first week under my guidance you will see and feel the improvement! Then as my weekly instructions arrive in your home you continue to rebuild, renew and "overhaul" your body. By the end of three months, you are the owner of a powerful body that you will be proud to display.

People will notice the ruddy glow of health in your face, the sparkle in your clear eyes, your broad shoulders, and they will seek your company. You will be the fellow who walks off with the prettiest girl and best job while others wonder how you did it!

These Secrets Have Helped Thousands

Write your name and address carefully on the coupon below. I'll send you a copy of my new book, *Everlasting Health and Strength*. It reveals the secrets that changed me from a 7-stone flat-chested weakling into a husky fellow who twice won the title of "The World's Most Perfectly Developed Man" against all comers! And it shows how I can build you into an *Atlas Champion* the same way.

ARE YOU UNDERWEIGHT?

I'll add pounds of muscles where they are needed! Are you fat in spots? I'll show you how to pare down to fighting trim. And with the big muscles and powerful, evenly developed body that my "*Dynamic-Tension*" method so quickly gives you. I'll also give you through-and-through health—health that digs down into your system and banishes constipation, indigestion and similar conditions that rob you of the good things of life.

I'VE NO USE FOR APPARATUS

I haven't any need for apparatus. I don't dose you or doctor you. "*Dynamic-Tension*" is all I need. It's my natural tested method for developing real men inside and out. It distributes added pounds of powerful muscles over your body, gets rid of surplus fat, and gives the vitality, strength and pep that win you the admiration of every woman and respect of any man. Get my book, *Everlasting Health and Strength*. Post my coupon today. Gamble a stamp to prove I can make YOU a new man!

GET FREE BOOK NOW...

PUPIL'S 7-INCH CHEST EXPANSION AMAZES R.A.F. DOCTOR

" I was passed grade one by an R.A.F. Medical Board on Tuesday. The Doctor who measured my chest said it was the best expansion he has seen for a long time, and he examined fifty every day. From right down to fully expanded the expansion was 7 inches. I am developing my body beautifully now and shall always be grateful to you."

Your pupil,—D.R.P. (Glam.)

Send for FREE BOOK

It tells you all about my "*Dynamic-Tension*" method, and how it has made big muscled men out of run-down specimens. It shows you from actual photos, how I have developed my pupils to the same perfectly balanced proportions of my own physique. What my system did for me and hundreds of others it can do for you, too. Don't keep on being only half the man you CAN be! Find out what I can do for you. Where shall I send your copy of *Everlasting Health and Strength*?

Post the coupon TO-DAY to: CHARLES ATLAS (Dept. 145/Q), 2 Dean Street, London, W.1.

NOTE *This is not a studio picture but an actual untouched snapshot.*

CHARLES ATLAS (Dept. 145/Q), 2 Dean St., London, W.1

I want the proof that your system of "*Dynamic Tension*" will make a New Man of me. Send me your book, "*Everlasting Health and Strength*," and full details of your amazing 7-DAY TRIAL OFFER.

NAME ....
(Please print or write plainly)

ADDRESS ....

"Sport," with which is incorporated "Seven," 13th year of publication, Vol. 13, No. 164. Published weekly by Topical Publishing Co. Ltd., 149 Fleet Street, E.C.4 (Central 3349). Printed by Hardy Press Ltd., Branksome, Bournemouth. All features are copyright and must not be reproduced without permission of the proprietors. Registered at the G.P.O. as a newspaper. Agents for overseas: Gordon & Gotch Ltd., Continental Publishers and Distributors.

MR GLUM: And it was then, Ted, I realized Eth was right. That boy is too dependent on me. He's got to leave home. But – will he do it?

LANDLORD: Well, why don't you just turf him out? Tell him to clear off out of it, don't come back.

MR GLUM: You're missing the point, Ted. He has to leave *voluntary*. Of his own free-wheel. And the only way to achieve that is to stop his idolizing of me. Make him see me in a different light. Make him, if necessary, dislike me. Even – despise me.

LANDLORD: Well, that shouldn't be difficult.

MR GLUM: It won't, if your nephew will help, Ted. Eth and me have got a plan to make Ron see me different – but it does demand your nephew's cooperation. So, Ted, give me time to get back and have a talk with Ron. Then send your nephew round in his sailor's uniform. And tell him this is what he's got to do . . .

As Mr Glum starts explaining – music – and we go forward in time to the Glums' sitting-room.

The three of them are arguing.

RON: *(firmly)* No, it's no use, Dad. I'm not going to leave home. I want to stay with you.

ETH: But, Ron –

RON: No, Eth. I don't think it's proper for a son to leave his father. Especially when they're related.

MR GLUM: All right, Ron, all right. In that case, you force me to reveal the secret wot I promised your dear mother I would never diverge. *(Deep breath)* Ron – I am not your father.

RON: Not – ? Oh, Dad, of course you're my father. I can smell the beer from here.

MR GLUM: I am *not* your father!

RON: You are, Dad.

ETH: Ron, please don't argue with your father when he says he is not your father.

MR GLUM: Ron, this is a serious moment. Let me tell you the truth as to where you came from.

RON: *(embarrassed)* Oh, Dad, you told me! All about that shop in Heaven.

MR GLUM: But what I'm giving you now is facts. You are not the progeny of my groins. Your mother and me opened the door one night and – there you were. Left on our doorstep. Now do you see what you really are?

RON: A milk-bottle?

MR GLUM: No relation at all! A nothing to me. So I'm no relation to you! See?

132

ETH: There, Ron. Does that change your feelings towards Mr Glum at all?

RON: *(soberly)* It – it certainly does, Eth.

ETH: Then would you like to ring up Murchison's again? I mean, seeing that Mr Glum's not your father now.

RON: He's not, is he?

ETH: No, Ron.

RON: He's – he's like nothing at all to me.

ETH: Yes, Ron.

RON: And I'm – I'm nothing at all to him.

ETH: Nothing, Ron.

RON: . . . And yet, he brought me up like I was his own son! *(Emotion)* Mr Glum, I'll never leave you now!

MR GLUM: Strike a light!

RON: I admire you more than ever, Mr Glum. All I want is to spend the rest of my life here at your –

MR GLUM: Will you belt up!

RON: Yes, Mr Glum.

MR GLUM: Ron – you've forced me to unveil the second half of my secret. Not only are you not my son but – something else.

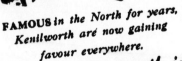
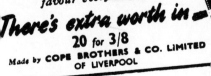

RON: I'm not your daughter either?

MR GLUM: Something even more poignant . . . I did have a real son.

ETH: (over-reacting) No! Oh, I can't believe it! Oh, no!

MR GLUM: Careful, Dame Ethel. Yes, I had a real son. One I took you in as a replacement for. My – my Theodore. He ran away to sea at the age of five.

RON: Five?

MR GLUM: They had smaller boats in those days.

RON: But even so, how could a five-year-old – ?

MR GLUM: Will you let me finish! Cor! He chooses now to start asking intelligent questions! My Theodore, he ran away to sea and I've never heard from him since. But this I know. Were he ever to walk through that door – he is the only one I'd want to love and cherish and take care of!

RON: Quite right, too. It must be very painful to walk through a door.

MR GLUM: Nobody else would matter if my Theodore came back. I'd – hark!

ETH: What, Mr Glum?

MR GLUM: Do I hear a knock on the door?

RON: No.

MR GLUM: (louder) Do I hear a knock on the door? A knock on the perishing – ? (A knock on the front door is heard and he starts back in elaborate surprise) That's a knock on the door! Who could be knocking on my door at this hour?

RON: Almost anybody. It's only four o'clock in the afternoon.

ETH: Oh, Ron. Go and open it and see.

RON: Right ho, Eth.

Ron leaves and we hear the front door opened.

MR GLUM: You know, Eth, if he does leave me I don't think I'm going to be as broken-hearted as I expected.

Ron re-enters, followed by George in his sailor's uniform.

RON: Dad, it's a sailor!

MR GLUM: A sailor! What ship is he from?

RON: Archie Les.

MR GLUM: Eh?

RON: That's what he's got on his hat.

ETH: Ron, that's Achilles.

MR GLUM: Achilles! The ship *he* sailed away on! Eth, it's him! It's him!

GEORGE: (repeating what he's been told to say) Hallo. After all this time – here I am!

MR GLUM: I can't believe it! *(Sob)* Oh, my wandering boy! Where hast thou bin?

RON: I went to open the door.

MR GLUM: Not you! This one. He's come back! In my old age, he hath returned! Oh, my heart is swelling to bursting.

ETH: It's like a miracle!

MR GLUM: *(eyes filled with tears)* Let me look at you! Ron, do you know who this is? Do you know who it is?!

RON: Yes.

MR GLUM: Are you sure?

RON: Oh yes. It's the nephew of the man in the pub.

ETH AND MR GLUM: Eh?

RON: We were at school together. His name's George.

GEORGE: I tried to tell Uncle Ted, but —

MR GLUM: *(baffled snarl)* Oh, git aht! Out of here!

GEORGE: Don't be like that, Mr Glum. I put me uniform on special to —

MR GLUM: Aht of it, I say, before I — ! *Aht!*

As George exits hurriedly —

MR GLUM: *(blazing)* That does it, Eth! We've tried subtlety, we've tried conniving, but if they don't work, then the time for sterner measures has come. *(He goes to phone and dials)* Perhaps this'll give Ron a different picture of his father. If he refuses to be parted from me by normal methods, then — *(Into phone)* Hallo, Murchison Manufacturing? Personnel Manager, please.

RON: *(fear)* Oh, Dad, no! I won't go. I won't live away from you. I won't. You can't make me.

MR GLUM: No? *(Into phone)* Hallo, Personnel Manager? My name's Glum. That job away from home you offered my son? Is it still open? *Right!*

RON: *(fearfully)* Right what?

MR GLUM: *I'm* taking it!

On Ron's wail of distress, we bring up music and BLACKOUT.

The pub, night-time. Pub hubbub, over which:

LANDLORD: *(shouting)* All right, last drinks, please. Time, gentlemen, please. Act of Parliament. Here, Mr Glum – there's something I been meaning to ask you for some time.

MR GLUM: Well, that's very kind of you, Ted. I'll have a brown.

LANDLORD: No, Mr Glum, about that son of yours.

MR GLUM: You mean Ron? The one-man depressed area?

LANDLORD: That's 'im. Didn't he click for a raffle prize last month?

MR GLUM: *(nodding)* In the Labour Exchange Christmas Draw. Valuable prize, too. A seventeen and sixpenny voucher, cashable at one of them shops behind the canal.

LANDLORD: Which shop?

MR GLUM: The tattooist's.

LANDLORD: . . . He got a free tattoo?

MR GLUM: That he did, Ted. And what an emotional crisis that bit of tattooing then precipitated. Because, Ted *(darkly)*, you have no idea what he *had* tattooed!

LANDLORD: Oh . . . Mind you, I've read about that being done.

MR GLUM: I'm not talking about the location, I'm referring to the subject matter. On his forearm he had three words tattooed. And I cannot tell you what heartache and upset them words caused his fiancée, young Eth.

LANDLORD: Why, what'd they say?

MR GLUM: *(solemnly)* From the evening she glimpsed 'em she was a changed girl. She came rushing to me, and – oh, Ted! – absolutely distroffed she was . . . !

Music – and we hark back to the Glums' sitting-room, night-time.

Mr Glum is endeavouring to comfort a distraught Eth.

ETH: *(crying)* Oh, Mr Glum . . . it's just so dreadful, I can't believe it. My Ron – leading a double life!

MR GLUM: Now, Eth, you know that cannot be true. He can only just about lead a single life.

ETH: *(tearfully)* *You* explain it then! Why else should he have tattooed on his right arm the words – *(gulp, then a loud wail)* – 'I love Sue'! *'Sue'!!!* And *my* name's Eth!

She dissolves into gulping sobs.

MR GLUM: Oh, for heaven's sake, stop that crying. You're making my corns throb. Now, Eth, let's get it straight. How is it you happened to see this inscription on his forearm?

ETH: It was on the bus, while Ron was wearing that secondhand jacket you gave him. He took it off to see the time on his wristwatch.

MR GLUM: He took off the whole jacket?

ETH: The sleeves *are* a bit long.

MR GLUM: Well, that's what happens when you get a jacket off-the-peg. Specially while the cloakroom attendant is *watching*. So it was then you happened to glimpse the words, eh?

ETH: Right across his forearm bold as you like. In royal-blue lettering – 'I love Sue'!

MR GLUM: Well, does that really signify? This 'Sue' – she could be some film-star he's taken a fancy to. Or one of them singing sensations. After all, look at all the girls who've got the name 'Lonnie Donnegan' embroidered across their chest. You did yourself. Though in your case, it came halfway round your back.

ETH: Embroidery's different. *(Passionately)* This is tattooing. It's permanent. For life. The only name you *tattoo* on yourself is somebody you really *love*.

MR GLUM: I see . . . So you think 'Sue' must be someone he's having a love affair with? Eth, I just somehow can't believe it. My Ron – a wolf in cheap clothing?

ETH: *(voice rising)* Who *is* she? That's what I want to know! When's he been seeing her? What is she *to* him? *(Hysterically)* How many *more* are there?

MR GLUM: Now, Eth, let's keep our sense of proportion. *(Pondering)* 'Sue' . . . 'Sue' . . . Not really a name you hear much round these parts. All the youngsters in this part of the world have got names like Claudette or Yana, or Car-ole. Except the boys, of course. But 'Sue' . . . that's really more of an *old-fashioned* name, isn't it?

ETH: *(horror)* An *older* woman? Oh!! That makes it even worse! Your Ron is playing fast-and-loose with a woman old enough to be his mother!

MR GLUM: *(placatory)* Now, Eth, hang on!

ETH: The slyness! The deceit! Him telling us he spends his afternoons just quietly leaning up against the Labour Exchange wall – when all the time . . ! Heaven knows what he's really leaning up against.

MR GLUM: Now, just control yourself. It's no purpose served getting overwrung. *(Grimly)* I'll find out who this Sue is! Leave that to me, Eth. I know Ron. I shall elicit the information obliquely.

ETH: How?

MR GLUM: I'll *bash* it out of him.

ETH: No! No, that you won't do. *(Struggling with her emotion)* I – I have my *pride*, Mr Glum.

MR GLUM: All right, *you* bash it out of him.

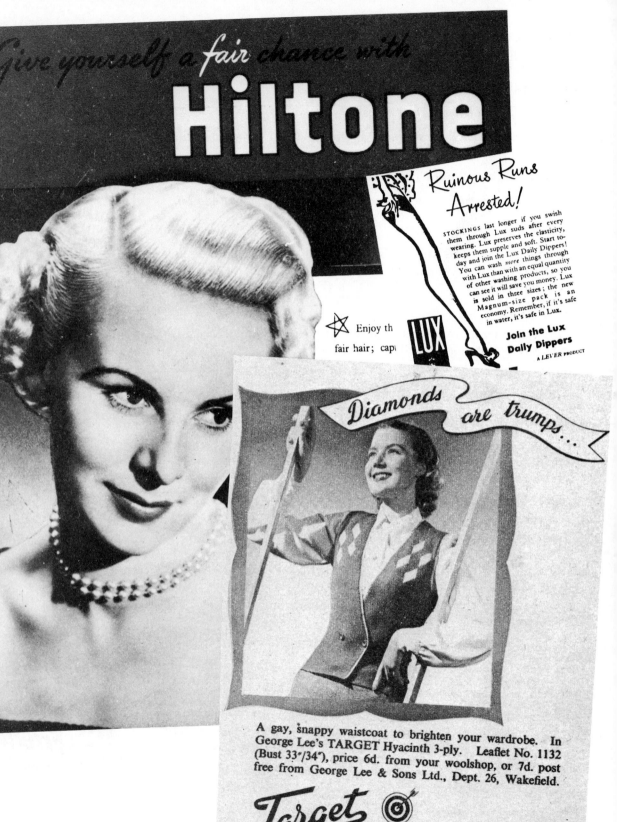

ETH: (*shakes her head*) I want to give him the chance to confess it off his own bat. I'll just lead the subject round and – let him tell me voluntary. So, if you'll be kind enough to leave us alone here after tea, I'll use my feminine wiles.

MR GLUM: (*furtively inspecting her*) Wiles?

ETH: You'll see, Mr Glum. (*Fiercely*) From now on, it's woman against woman.

MR GLUM: And may the best man win.

As he pats her hand – music – and we move on to the Glums' sitting-room after tea.

Ron and Eth are on the sofa.

ETH: (*disingenuous*) Oh, Ron . . . isn't it odd? I've had a tune running round in my head all evening and I just can't think of the title. I wonder if you know it, Ron?

RON: No, Eth.

ETH: I haven't *told* you it yet, beloved. It goes like this. (*She da-das significantly the tune of 'Sweet Sue'*) Do you know it?

RON: Yes, Eth.

ETH: What is it?

RON: It's the one that goes – (*he hums 'Sweet Sue'*)

ETH: Oh, never mind, Ron. Let me put what's in my mind another way. Ron, darling, lately I have a sort of feeling you've been a little – withdrawn.

RON: Not really, Eth. I've still got one and nine left in.

ETH: I wasn't talking in the Post Office sense, dearest. I mean – you're sort of withdrawn *into* yourself.

RON: Oh. Well, that's the sleeves on this jacket.

ETH: (*casting about*) Well, let me put it yet another way, Ron . . . Quite often you find that young *girls* get very romantic about an older and more mature type of *man*. Know what I mean?

RON: No, Eth.

ETH: Well . . . Rossano Brazzi, Ron.

RON: Oh . . . Goodnight then, Eth.

ETH: It's not a farewell, Ron. It's a Greek film star. All crinkles round the eyes and at the temples. And the funny thing is, it's the *young* girls he attracts. (*Carefully*) Now, would it be true to say this also happens the other way round?

RON: Oh, I shouldn't think so, Eth.

ETH: (*pouncing*) Why not?

RON: Well, I doubt whether he's got any crinkles there.

ETH: (*patiently*) Ron, wouldn't it be possible for a boy – of your age – to be similarly attracted by an older *woman*?

RON: Well —

ETH: Before you answer that, Ron, let me add that personally I think it *is* possible and that a boy could well have a temporary infatuation, *but* — as long as he realizes it is *only* an infatuation and he confesses it of his *own free will* to whoever he might be duty-bound to confess it *to* — there is absolutely no harm, and whoever he confesses it to *should* forgive him and *would*. So, now . . . what were you about to say?

RON: . . . Eth, I — I have a confession to make.

ETH: *(eagerly)* . . . Yes, Ron?

RON: I didn't understand a word of that.

ETH: *(despair)* Oh, *Ron!!!*

Mr Glum enters the room.

MR GLUM: All right, Eth, I'll take over.

RON: Dad?

MR GLUM: I couldn't help overhearing Eth's conversation, Ron, on account of I was listening. Now, Ron, the time for shilly-shallying is past. You have caused your fiancée much mental anguish and torment. It is now up to you to answer a straight question. *How do you come to have the words 'I love Sue' tattooed on your arm?*

RON: *(pause, then slowly)* Oh . . . You've found out.

ETH: Yes, Ron.

MR GLUM: *(finger tapping)* Ron — I'm waiting for your answer.

RON: Dad, I — I can't tell you.

ETH: Please, Ron.

MR GLUM: Ron, it's no good pulling your cap down over your face. We're still here. So out with it. Why have you got 'I love Sue' engraved on yourself?

RON: Dad, I — I *can't* tell you. I just can't.

ETH: Why not?

RON: Because I — I feel so ashamed. I was — foolish and, and . . . *weak*. It started out as just a bit of fun but then .. . I don't know what came over me.

ETH: Oh, Ron.

RON: Don't ask me to say any more. I — I won't. If you'll excuse me, I'll — I'll go and take the dog out for a walk. *(He leaves)*

ETH: Oh, Mr Glum, he's — he's terribly disturbed, isn't he?

MR GLUM: He must be, Eth. We haven't got a dog.

ETH: But I must know more than he's told us, Mr Glum. I *must*!!

MR GLUM: Well, you won't get it out of *him*, Eth. I know Ron. You can threaten all you like now, it won't make one Aida of difference. When he's got his obstinate face on, you can't shift him. I know that from trying to get him to finish his greens.

ETH: You mean we'll *never* find out who this Sue is?

MR GLUM: Oh, I'm not saying that, Eth. (*Thinking hard*) There is one other person who *might* know who she is. It's a slim chance. But, as the old adage says, a shot in the dark is worth two in the bush. Come on, Eth.

As he pulls the bewildered Eth to her feet – music – and the scene changes to the tattooist's parlour, afternoon.

The tattooist is showing his book of sample-tattoos to Mr Glum and Eth.

TATTOOIST: Yes, sir, 'the Rembrandt of the electric needle', that's what they call me. In this book you'll find everything from a portrait of King Edward VII to a trellis-work pattern of flowering dog roses stretching from clavicle to tummy button.

MR GLUM: Yes, highly ornamental, I'm sure. But we haven't really come here with the object of being artistically perforated.

ETH: We're enquiring as regards a Mr Ronald Glum, whom you did an inscription on his forearm.

TATTOOIST: Ronald – ? Oh, yes, the free voucher. Yes, I recall that client now. He had to take his jacket off to shake hands.

ETH: Mr Peasglove, would you happen to know why Ron wanted that *particular* name?

TATTOOIST: Most certainly I do. We talked it over fully while I was putting a new needle in. I'd worn out the other one on my previous client, you see. What a lovely job *that* was. A full-sized multi-coloured Lonsdale Belt stretching right round the waist.

MR GLUM: Lummy, that must have cost a bit.

TATTOOIST: (*dignity*) She has plenty of money.

ETH: Mr Peasglove, please. Would you please tell us everything that Ron told you?

TATTOOIST: (*shocked*) Oh no. I'm afraid the relationship of tattooist and tattooed is like doctor and patient.

MR GLUM: But this could mean the whole future happiness of two young people.

TATTOOIST: I'm sorry. To betray a professional confidence is tantamount to breaking my Royal School of Needlework oath.

MR GLUM: (*menacing*) All right, mate. If you won't talk willingly – (*He picks up the tattooing needle, seizes tattooist*)

ETH: Mr Glum – !

MR GLUM: (*savagely*) How'd you like to have profanities scrawled all over you?

TATTOOIST: No! No! Help!

Week ending February 9, 1952   EVERY THURSDAY   3½ ID.

Picturegoer

THE NATIONAL FILM WEEKLY

GLORIA GRAHAME

BRITISH FILMS GET A SHINER — *see centre*

The shop bell tinkles off.

ETH: Mr Glum, there's someone in the shop.

RON'S VOICE: *(calling)* Mr Tattooist! You there, Mr Tattooist? I want you to take back my tattoo and return my seventeen and six. *He enters the back parlour.* Mr Tattoo – Dad! Eth! *(Face falls)* So he's told you.

ETH: Well, actually, Ron, he refused to betr – oooogh!!

Mr Glum has stabbed Eth with the needle.

MR GLUM: Sorry, Eth – did it accidentally enter your thigh? My apologies. *(To Ron)* Yes, Ron, He told us everything. But we'd like to hear the story again in *your* words.

RON: Well, it's – it's nothing to be proud of. You see, when I came here with the voucher, Mr Tattooist asked me what did I want to have tattooed.

TATTOOIST: Seventeen and six only entitles you to a short inscription.

RON: For seventeen and six I was only entitled to a short inscription. Well, Dad – I couldn't think of one.

TATTOOIST: So I helped him. I told him that what people *usually* have tattooed is 'I love' – then the name of – *(coyly)* – the object of their affection.

RON: And I had to be honest about it. When it comes to loving, you must tell the truth.

ETH: *(sadly)* And so the name you decided on, Ron, was this – *(bravely)* – 'Sue'!

RON: That's what I'm so ashamed about, Eth. Like I said, I was weak and foolish.

MR GLUM: Why?

RON: Well – he got as far as S-U-E and then I – fainted!

MR GLUM: Flaked out?

RON: He was on my funny bone.

MR GLUM: Just a minute, just a minute, Ron. Do you mean that 'I love Sue' is not the complete message?

RON: No, Dad.

ETH: Then perhaps, Ron, you'll tell us at last the *full* name of this great love of yours.

Ron shuffles his feet.

MR GLUM: Go on. 'I love –'?

RON: . . . *(pause, then, tenderly)* 'Suet pudding!'

MR GLUM: *(rage)* Suet – ? Gimme that needle!

RON: *(simultaneously)* No, Dad, no! Oogh! OOOOH!

As Mr Glum endeavours to embroider Ron with tattoos – playout music and
BLACKOUT.